T0118156

The Night,
and the Rain,
and the River

the night, and the rain, and the river

22 stories... edited by liz prato

with letterpress art by clare carpenter

Jan Baross, Gail Bartley, Victoria Blake, Alisha Churbe, Sage Cohen, Ellen Davidson Levine, Steve Denniston, Trevor Dodge, Gregg Kleiner, Christi Krug, Kathleen Lane, Dylan Lee, Margaret Malone, Matthew Robinson, Joanna Rose, Lois Rosen, Jackie Shannon Hollis, Domi Shoemaker, Scott Sparling, Tammy Lynne Stoner, Jennifer Williams, and Cindy Williams Gutiérrez

FOREST AVENUE PRESS
Portland, Oregon

This is a work of fiction. Names, characters, places, and incidents are products of the authors' imaginations or are used fictitiously. Any resemblance to actual events, locales, or persons, living or dead, is entirely coincidental.

© 2014 by Liz Prato

All rights reserved. No portion of this publication may be reproduced in any form, with the exception of reviewers quoting short passages, without the written permission of the publisher.

978-0-9882657-5-2

Library of Congress Control Number: 2013958328

First edition 2014
Printed in the United States of America
by Forest Avenue Press LLC
Portland, Oregon

2 3 4 5 6 7 8 9

Cover design: Gigi Little
Letterpress art: Clare Carpenter, Tiger Food Press
Interior design: Laura Stanfill
Copy editor: Annie Denning Hille

Distributed by Legato Publishers Group

Forest Avenue Press is grateful to Oregon Literary Arts for the 2014
publishing fellowship that helped finance the publication of this anthology.

Forest Avenue Press LLC
6327 SW Capitol Highway, Suite C
PMB 218
Portland, OR 97239
forestavenuepress.com

Contents

In Which Liz Prato, the Writer Interviews Liz Prato, the Editor

LP WRITER: CAN YOU tell our readers how you became the editor for *The Night, and the Rain, and the River*?

LP Editor: One day Laura Stanfill and I were driving out to Sandy, Oregon, where we were both reading at an event. Laura had started Forest Avenue Press a few months earlier and had just opened submissions for quiet novels. I was impressed with and excited by her vision for the press and wanted to be involved somehow. But I was already busy with teaching and writing and my day job, and I don't consider novels to be my forte. So, I assumed there wasn't a way for me to be involved, other than as a supporter. Then, during that drive to Sandy, Laura totally surprised me by asking me to edit a short story anthology for the press.

LP Writer: So, did you say yes right away?

LP Editor: No. Laura said I should think about it, and I said

I should think about it. We went to the reading and both read and heard other writers read. And then, as we were driving home, I said, "I thought about it and I'm in."

LP Writer: Just like that? No reservations? Is this going to be another one of those stories where you end up tearing your hair out and asking, *Why didn't I think this through?*

LP Editor: I had zero reservations. I couldn't come up with a convincing downside—which I realize is the set-up for all comedies of errors. But seeing how neither of us are Noel Coward characters (even though Laura frequently dresses like one), I decided to forge ahead.

LP Writer: Okay, so it's Day One of the open submission period. What were your expectations?

LP Editor: I had no idea what to expect. I couldn't even hazard a guess at how many stories we'd receive and who they'd be from and what they'd be about. That's what was astonishing and frightening about this process: we committed to publishing a book in May 2014, but we hadn't the foggiest idea what the content would be or who the authors would be. It's backwards from how most publishers work with a single-author title. It was a giant leap of faith that somehow we'd actually have a great book at the end.

LP Writer: What was the process of reading and choosing stories like for you?

LP Editor: I surprised myself. I assumed I would be really impatient with stories that were less advanced . . .

LP Writer: Yes, I've seen you do that before. You seem to take it oddly personally.

LP Editor: And it *was* frustrating, but only because I wanted to discover really good stories. You always hear this cynical take that all editors are immediately looking for a reason to reject the stories they read, and I assumed that would be the case for me. Instead, I was really bummed when a story didn't work, because I so badly wanted it to. Not just for me and the anthology, but also for the author. In almost every case, I could feel that the author really believed in the story. They weren't just phoning it in.

LP Writer: Did you have certain themes you were searching for among the submissions?

LP Editor: No, I had this idea that the themes would emerge organically. That they'd just show themselves. At one point, we had several submissions about dealing with a loved one's ashes. And we were like, "Jeez, are we going to publish a whole anthology about ashes? About death?"

LP Writer: A lot of my writing is about death. I'd think it would be tempting—and pretty easy—for you to create an entire anthology around that theme.

LP Editor: Well, just because *you* write a lot about death doesn't mean the whole world wants to read two dozen stories in a row about death, you know? Instead, I just picked strong stories that spoke to my heart and I thought would speak to other people's hearts as well. At first I wasn't sure of the themes. And when I looked at the stories I had accepted—twenty-two of them—I was, like, "Okay: we have a goose, and an arsonist, and drug addicts and mothers and fathers and adulterers," which sounds pretty random, but they all had one theme. They were all about longing to belong. To another's heart, to family, to oneself. Which is perfectly in line with the vision of the press —as well as my personal ideals: that we are all a part of this beautiful bigger entity and can help each other along the way. I hope that's what these stories do. I hope they help other people feel less alone.

LP Writer: Is there anything else you'd like to say before we finish up?

LP Editor: Thank you all for writing and for reading and for being true to yourself and others. It's why we are here, slowly spinning around a brightly burning star.

To read the full text of this interview, visit the bonus web-only feature at forestavenuepress.com.

Saving the Animals

Margaret Malone

MY BOSS BARB IS wearing her tailored black raincoat and underneath are her pajamas. Her short gray hair is blowing in the wind, almost straight up. Her hands are cupped around her mouth in order to send her voice out as far as possible, past the walking path and toward the bay. It is almost midnight and impossible to see anything or anyone out in the black water.

"Goo-ooose," she calls.

This is what she's named him. Goose.

Barb looks to where I am under the streetlight leaning against my folks' car, my arms hugging my body to keep warm. Her voice calls down to me.

"Christ, Mindy. Do something," she says. "Help me yell." She turns back toward the dark water and calls his name again. Her voice eaten up by the wind.

As always, she is exasperated. She cannot understand why everyone isn't always as enthusiastic as she is to do whatever it is that needs to be done.

I scramble up the embankment, over the vegetation, my feet

unsteady on the slippery leaves and hard roots, and then I am up and onto the bike path in the freezing dark.

I'VE BEEN WORKING FOR Barb for sixteen years, as long as I've been out of college. I know her so well I do not need her to tell me what she's thinking because her voice is already going in my head, what she wants, when she needs it, who she wants me to call. Even so, I never saw this thing with Goose coming.

Barb is especially exasperated when it comes to my social life. To my face she tries to be encouraging, urging me to stop being such a homebody and "get out there," as if *there* was a specific place I needed to go where at last I'd find myself surrounded by all the men I couldn't manage to meet on my own. But away from my face I've heard her say other, more direct, things. I overheard her talking to her son on the phone more than once. *Depressed,* she said. *Dependent,* she said. *Desperate to be married.* She said, *Well, she could be attractive if she'd color her hair, lose a few pounds, and wear some blush.* She said, *No, I certainly don't want you asking her out.*

At the very least, she wanted me to spend time out of the house, with anybody other than my parents. But to that I say— Yes, well look at me here: I am out now. I am spending time with someone in the middle of the night at the foot of a bridge looking for a goose. This is an excellent example of why I prefer to stay home.

Home for me is the attic apartment of my parents' house. We call it the attic but really it's a weird addition they threw on top of the house when I was in high school—just a project so my dad and my brother Louis could spend time together. They built it themselves and it is obvious they didn't get a permit or consult a professional because the roof leaks when it rains and the floor is so thin my folks and I talk to each other right through it. What else I don't like is that the only entrance is through the main house, through the living room, past the kitchen and up the bare wood stairs. That said, they only charge four hundred a month. All in all it's a pretty good deal. Most nights I can hear them underneath me, my family, like an ocean, because they make so much goddamn noise. They yell when they talk, like seamen coordinating in a storm. TV is the only way to drown their voices out.

I am an embarrassment to my father because I'm the last of my cousins not to marry. I mean the women. In my family, nobody cares if the men don't marry. The men are allowed to stay home indefinitely, mooch off the parents, and live like slobs. But the women. I'm talking about the women. The only other single cousin, Mara, was just married last month. She stood up at the altar next to a dog of a man and said okay instead of I do. When the floor cleared for their first dance she took her time getting up there, slugged a shot of Jameson with me, strapped her shoes back on, and walked into the hazy spotlight. Just like that, she's a wife.

Barb says it's because I'm not putting myself out there. I try to listen to what she says because she's my boss and, even though she yells a lot, I respect her. She's really made something of herself, head of her own design company, and she goes out of her way to support me. But I also don't listen too hard because she's not married either, not anymore, and also she's a little loony like how right now she has me out here in the middle of the night calling for a goose so he can come back home. Home being the business park pond where the goose used to live before Barb drove him down here this afternoon to the foot of the bridge to save him.

These are the times I wished more than one person worked for Barb. Once a month and at tax time the accountant comes in and sits at one of the empty desks in back by the copier. Otherwise it is me and her and nobody else.

IT WASN'T JUST THAT Goose was friendly or that Barb was walking down to the pond at lunch to feed him popcorn. It was that Goose started to come looking for Barb. If she missed a day, Goose wandered up to the big picture window of her office that looks out over the business park pond and trees. He'd scuttle up the grassy hill and over to her window and peck his bill on the broad clear glass to say hello.

She'd shriek like George Clooney was out there. "Mindy, Goose is back."

It's true that the window was a large wall of glass at ground level, but even so, I didn't understand how a goose could see through any window. They have these little round eyes, and each eye is facing out on the opposite side of their face.

It says a lot about me that Barb could get a goose and I can't even get a man.

I DON'T THINK WHAT happened today was planned. It was just a normal Tuesday at first. Coffee, email from clients, Barb barking for one file or another. As always, Barb had been out first thing that morning to feed popcorn to the geese, and now that it was almost lunch Goose walked up the shallow grass slope to peck his bill at Barb's window. My desk was just outside her door, and because I didn't have a window and there was nothing to see, listening was what I got good at.

My face was in the MacKenzie file.

The wheels of Barb's leather office chair squawked. "Shit," Barb said. "Here comes Raul."

Raul was the security guard for the building and he was not a fan of the geese, and definitely not of Goose, and particularly not of the relationship that had bloomed between Barb and Goose.

I heard the familiar dull knocking of goose bill against glass. Then Barb's voice. "Shoo," she said. "Get."

I pretended to keep my mind on Mr. MacKenzie's file.

Now it sounded like Barb was knocking against the glass with her knuckles. Barb's voice. "You're a little shit!"

Barb charged out of her office, passing my desk so quickly the stack of correspondence in the MacKenzie file fluttered.

"That shit," she said.

I pretended to keep working until she was out the front door then I hustled into her office to watch through the big picture window.

There was Raul, shaped like a yam with arms and legs. His tiny eyes and clenched lips overtaken like an avalanche by his big mound of a head. His face mostly stubbly flesh with features designed for a much smaller man. Barb's muted mouth opened and closed, her eyes scrunched into tiny slivers, crow's feet erupting from their corners. Her nude stockings and black high heels right up against his black security boots, feet wide apart. The tips of her fingers poked into his doughboy chest. He smiled his tight little security guard smile through Barb's assault, but I could see his worry underneath—Barb's love of that goose was unpredictable in its ferocity. His eyes jumped to find mine through the window and I shook my head. No way, my eyes said back. I'm not about to help you, buddy.

I knew Raul. We had graduated from the same high school and he was mean then too. One time junior year he asked me if I'd like to go to the winter formal with him and when I said I would he said I bet you would but I wouldn't want to go with you. That was a long time ago, I know, but now that he's a yam in uniform, I don't mind to see him humiliated publicly by the wrath of Barb's seismic voice.

By the time Barb returns, I'm back at my desk creating a new client folder. Her cheeks are flushed from yelling.

Barb says, "Now he's saying it's not him. It's the cleaning crew."

The phone rings and I answer. "Good morning. Barbara Trevor Design."

Barb keeps talking. "He says the cleaning crew says it's

because of his shit up here by the window. They don't like cleaning up all that shit."

"That would be me I guess," I say to the phone.

Barb says, "Then Raul threatened him. Said don't get too attached. Said sometimes these geese, they just disappear."

I say, "We are very happy with our current copy machine. Thank you." I hang up.

"Can I go to lunch now?" I say.

EVERY DAY I EAT my lunch at the pond, a cheese and bologna sandwich and corn chips, unless it's raining or too cold. There are three benches by the pond and one is the one in the shade where the geese don't poop much. That's where I sit. Even though I know the pond is fake and made by the business park architects, I still find it peaceful. There are little birch trees and green grass and the small lake the size of a parking lot with the fountain spitting up in the middle.

The geese usually come visit at my bench while I eat but I don't feed them and they don't bother me and I play a game where I try to guess which one is Goose.

The sandwich was down the hatch and I was snacking on chips when Barb out of nowhere stood next to me. She was wearing her tailored black raincoat and carrying a dirty green towel. Her purse was over her shoulder.

"Are you going home for lunch?" I said.

Barb said, "I'm going to pull my car around front. I want you to grab him from behind."

Initially I thought she was talking about Raul. I don't think I could get my arms around Raul if I tried.

She said, "He'll come over when he sees this." She pulled a bag of popcorn out of her giant mouth of a purse. Her other arm extended toward me with the dirty towel. "And you'll need this."

Barb tossed it next to me on the bench. I did not reach for

the towel. Technically, I was still at lunch.

Barb shook the bag of popcorn like a pom-pom and called out across the pond to him. "Hi Goose. Here comes my Goose. What a good goose you are. What a good goose. Do you want to go for a ride in my car? Yes you do. Yes you do."

Sure enough, the gaggle tramped toward us, their geese breasts stuck out proud. I stood up from the bench. My corn chips fell off my lap and the animals swarmed and pecked at the pile.

"This one. See the difference?" Barb said. "He has a particular intelligence." She pointed at one as his neck extended and he pecked the ground with his black bill.

Barb said, "I'll be one second." She handed me the bag of popcorn and hurried toward her car in the lot behind me.

My heart beat my pulse loud in my ears and I understood it to be saying, *You do not want to steal a goose.*

There he was at my feet. Pecking bill. The dirty towel under my arm.

Familiar pit in my gut that said no when I did not. My quiet voice croaked out a call.

"Good Goose," I said. My hand tossed him a puffy kernel. "Good boy." I didn't know how to talk to a goose.

Barb's engine turned over in the parking lot, and Goose looked over toward the noise like maybe he did want to go. She threw the passenger door open from inside and leaned her body over the armrest.

She yelled from the car. She said, "Grab him from behind and stick him right here." Her hand patted the seat.

"Shit," I said to myself. I do not normally swear. Not ever. Across the pond, the UPS guy Gary hopped out of his truck in his little brown shorts and waved to me on his way into the building. I waved back. Normal, normal, my wave said. Everything normal.

My eyes met Goose's eyes. I took a long look at him. His

long black legs and pretty feathers that from far away look black and brown but up close like this are actually lots of colors, which remind me of sand and copper and coal.

I held the towel open like wings and whispered *Sorry* and lunged for Goose, grabbing him from behind.

His wings had sharp elbows. I hugged him to my chest like a squiggly baby.

He clucked and honked, his wings tried to flap, bits of his feathers floated up and stuck to my lips.

Ahead of me stretched the grassy expanse that led to Barb's car, passenger door flung open, parked sideways in the handicapped spot. The distance elongated in front of me with each step I took. I had no idea how long it would take to get there. It might take forever. It occurred to me pond geese might be protected by some kind of law. It occurred to me I could go to jail, and then seemed certain: I'm going to go to jail. I'll be in jail for kidnapping a big feathery bird and no man will ever marry me. I will never be a bride. I'll die an old maid like Aunt Louisa, hiding Snickers wrappers in my couch cushion and eating dinner at four in the afternoon.

"Looking good," Barb said.

That's when I felt it on my wrist, warm and wet. He'd pooped on me, which, when I thought about it, seemed like an appropriate response to being kidnapped.

I knelt into the open door of the passenger side and plopped Goose in.

Barb said, "You poor thing. You're covered in poop." She was talking to the goose. She held him down while I shut his door and climbed into the backseat.

Goose was weirdly calm once he was in the car.

He sat in the front seat sideways just like I'd left him, the dirty towel with feathers and poop around his feet. He was facing Barb, turning his head left and then right and then left and then right.

"See," Barb said. "I told you."

I wasn't sure if she was talking to me or the goose.

"He knows we're trying to help him," she said. "He wants our help."

I stayed quiet in the back.

EVERY TIME I'M IN Barb's BMW I'm amazed by the interior. Black leather seats and a fancy navigation system with maps and buttons and lights that look like the cockpit of a plane. If I had a fancy car, I'd never put a goose in it but Barb is funny like that. Borrowing her car to drive ten blocks to pick up sandwiches for a client meeting is out of the question, but she'll let a pooped-up goose ride shotgun.

The car flipped a U-turn and drove out of the lot.

Goose let out a loud honk.

"I know," Barb said.

He tried to fly at the windshield.

"I'm sorry," she said. "My poor baby."

Out my side window, the office park pond looked normal, the water feature in the center spitting water up into the air, the trees hanging over the sides of the pond. The stone benches empty. Everything like it was supposed to be. Just one goose short.

THE CAR WAS GOING slow through the streets of Foster City. We passed the big mall and the diner I like because they make good waffles. The radio was on, chatter about the stock market. The tick tick of Barb's blinker as she moved over a lane.

Goose aimed his long neck at the roof of the car. Let loose a low moo that climbed to a proper honk.

"Hold tight," Barb said. "We're almost there."

The BMW turned off Hillsdale Boulevard onto a small side street and entered one of the subdivisions built on top of the marsh. All of Foster City is built on marshland. Originally the marsh stretched between San Mateo and the bay, an intermediary between land and water. Then developers came through in the sixties and put cement over the marshland and built a bunch of look-alike houses and people moved in. Finally they slapped a bike path onto the perimeter of everything. It traces the edge of the manmade land so the people can jog and pedal and push strollers while looking out across all that water.

Barb picked a street and headed east/southeast according to her cockpit controls. We drove through the neighborhood. There were not a lot of trees. A woman my age in sweatpants stood next to an open minivan door yelling at someone inside. Farther down a knocked-over pink tricycle rested on its side in a broad cement driveway. A big white boat asleep under a blue tarp.

The street spit us out against the embankment below the bike path not too far from the foot of the long white San Mateo Bridge.

Barb parked her car against the sidewalk next to an incline of green vegetation. I could make out the bridge's rush of moving traffic, the sound in competition with the water on the other side of the incline lapping against the rocks.

The three of us sat in the quiet car.

I watched a seagull through the car window. It caught a rise of wind over the bay.

"I don't see any other geese," I said.

"That's ridiculous. Of course there are geese here. Geese love water. Why do you think they're always around that pond?" Barb said. "It's because of the water."

When Barb got out of the car I did too. She walked around to the passenger door and opened it wide. Goose erupted from the car in an awkward takeoff, one wing catching on the car frame. He hobbled to the embankment's incline of vegetation that separates the street from the bike path. Ruffled himself, shook his tail feathers, spread his wings as far as they'd open, and honked out one big cry.

Goose walked up the incline and we followed him. Barb in her black suit and black high heels. Me in my slacks and flats. My sweat staining the underarms of my work blouse.

The water lapped against the rocks. The traffic off a ways on the bridge. A bicyclist sped by me. A lady in red shorts was jogging farther down the path.

"I don't see any other geese," I said again.

Goose pecked his bill at the ground.

"Will you be okay here?" Barb said. "Do you think you can make some new friends?"

Goose spread his wings and flapped them around and laid them back against his chest.

"Well, all right then," Barb said. "Goodbye to you too."

On the return car ride it was very quiet. I sat in the back again. Radio on low, some kind of news. The car was like a crime scene, Goose's bunched up towel on the passenger seat, grassy wild poop smell. When Barb pulled into the office lot and parked, neither of us got out.

Big white clouds floated low in the blue sky. I could see them reflected in the mirrored windows of the office building.

"That's right, wasn't it?" she said. "What we did?"

A light wind tugged at the branches of the trees surrounding the pond.

"I guess," I said. "I don't know."

"Oh Jesus, Mindy. Have a fucking opinion sometimes." Barb blew her nose. Sniffed. I couldn't tell if she was crying or if her allergies were acting up.

I got out of the car and walked past the pond, the bench, the trees. The rest of the geese were on the other side of the grass now, pecking. Two were swimming together in the pond.

For the rest of the day we didn't say much. Even the phone

barely rang. I typed client letters on the computer and ate an old bag of peanut M&Ms I found at the back of my desk drawer. At the end of the day I called goodnight to Barb without poking my head in the door and I did not look over when I walked past the pond.

DEEP INTO MY NIGHTTIME ritual, I'm reading in bed, hand in an open bag of Milano cookies, my cat Roger asleep on his side at my feet. The phone rings. I share a land line with my parents downstairs, but I don't answer it because it's never for me.

My mom shouts through the floor.

"It's Barb," she says.

I PULL JEANS ON over my pajamas. Grab my purse and my dad's old heavy wool flannel shirt that I wear like a jacket and head downstairs. I can hear a TV talking behind my parents' bedroom door.

I put my head close to the shut door and listen, just to have a moment to myself.

I knock twice. I say, "It's me."

My dad says, "Duh."

My head pokes through the open door. I cannot see their faces, just two sets of feet poked up under bed covers facing the nightly news on the television screen.

I say, "I need to borrow the car. Is that okay?"

My dad says, "You'll never get a man to marry you with a boss like that. You might as well marry her instead."

My mom says, "My keys are on the entry table."

The furnace kicks on. Air pushed through the vents. Roger follows me down the stairs, his metal tag clanging with each step. Louis is where he always is, in the living room, feet in their socks, stretched out on Dad's brown corduroy recliner. Green field on the TV. Different colored outfits running from one side of the screen to the other. I grab Mom's keys from the entry table.

"You got a booty call?" Louis says.

"Very funny," I say. "I have to meet Barb."

"Mom and Dad think you're a lesbian, you know."

"Shut up, Louis," I say. "That's just Dad."

"I'm just saying," he says.

IT'S CHILLY AND THE fog is rolling in over the hills. My big flannel should be warm enough but the damn wind is blowing and my ears are cold. Barb is already up on the bike path calling for Goose. She's wearing her tailored black raincoat and underneath, like me, her pajamas. Her short gray hair is blowing in the wind, standing almost straight up. She is walking the paved path, visible and then not under the tall street lamps' umbrellas of light. Visible and then not. Visible and then not.

She spots me leaning against my folks' car and her voice yells down to me, exasperated as always. I climb up the incline of vegetation and head the opposite direction on the path, north along the water.

I can hear the sound of water against rock just past the path and a muffled angry truck horn from far off and everything in the bay is black except for the lights on the bridge trailing the seven miles to the other side of the bay where there is finally land again. Lights overhead blink red and white, reflected in the water from the sky, as a plane heads for SFO to land and empty out its passengers.

I'm alone except for Barb way behind me, everything dark except for the umbrellas of light. It feels good to be out here in nowhere by myself late at night.

Headed away from her, there is no way for me to hear Barb's voice. It doesn't matter. We will never find the goose. I know this. But for Barb's sake I try.

"Goose," I say. It's more of an insistent whisper.

"Goose. Goose. Goose."

The long white snaking bones of the bridge stretching over the black water. The blowing wind and quiet sky.

"Goose," I say. I am louder now.

What do I know. Maybe he's out there. Maybe I'm wrong.

"Goose!" I say again.

"Goose!" I use my whole voice.

And there. I see something. Is that him? That could be a goose, out a ways in the water, sailing the chop on top of the bay. I stop and listen. The sound of easy nighttime traffic, the bay's rhythmic touching to shore, the tall fingers of dry grass rustling together in the wind.

I stop calling his name.

Yes, that's enough. It's enough to think maybe.

More of What You Already Are

Gail Bartley

EVERY TIME AUBREY BURNS gets arrested, when he tells the cops his name they think he's being a smart ass until they look him up in their computers. Then they all have a big un-funny cop laugh—ha ha ha—which hurts Aubrey's feelings and is rude besides. He's wondered for years if his name is what makes him do these things. Or is it just the universe's way of calling a spade a spade? He knows he's a firebug, one-third of the homicidal triad, according to a book he stole from Barnes & Noble.

On the other two points of the killer's triangle, Aubrey's safe. He was just your average bed wetter (an occasional bad dream or too much pop) and grew out of that by age six. The closest he ever came to animal abuse was the time he left his dime store turtle paddling sad little circles in its plastic pond in the backyard, where he promptly forgot him until he tripped over the pond a week later. Being August, there was nothing left of the turtle but a tiny shrunken head poking stiffly from its shell. After all these years, Aubrey still feels awful about it, suggesting he's not a sociopath, either. Sociopaths (according to the book) commit horrible acts and never lose a wink of sleep. Aubrey, on the other hand, feels bad about practically everything in his life except setting fires, which make his heart pound like he's a rocket shooting toward the moon. He knows he should be sorry for all the damage he's done. He's really tried. Sat in the groups, done the exercises, swallowed the pills. But deep down, the only part of setting fires he truly regrets is getting caught.

His first memory of fire is the shuddering yellow dance of candles lighting up a birthday cake in a darkened room. What room, whose cake, he can't remember. His parents didn't bother with celebrating birthdays, so Aubrey knows it wasn't his. When she's sober, Aubrey's mother Marlene blames herself for his crimes. When she's not, she blames his dad, who never set fire to a thing but his cigarettes and the trash barrel out back. He ditched Aubrey and Marlene when Aubrey was only eight. Walked out the door one morning with his plaid thermos and never looked back.

Three months later, their garage burned down, full of Aubrey's dad's tools and his half-finished birdhouses. By the time the fire department arrived, flames were shooting twenty feet in the air. Neighbors hung around in little clumps, speculating on whether the pine tree beside the garage would ignite. Aubrey stood among them, transfixed by his secret and the snapping, radiant heat. He was clutching his Sting Ray bicycle with the deluxe banana seat which he'd bought himself with paper route money. Poor kid, thought the neighbors. First his dad leaves, now this. At least he didn't lose his bike.

Looking back on it later, Marlene remembered thinking it was odd that the bike, which Aubrey always kept in the garage, just happened to be out in the driveway that night. But, firebug or not, twenty years and who knows how many arrests later, when Aubrey gets locked up like he is just now, she visits him once a month, riding the prison shuttle bus with all the other sad mothers, grim wives, and pregnant girlfriends.

Aubrey wishes he had a girlfriend's visit to look forward to instead of his mother's, but he can barely get a date on account of being so shy. Self-doubt is Aubrey's very own noxious weed, rooting in every corner and choking out confidence, smothering opportunity. Being five foot two doesn't help, or add to a guy being taken seriously, especially in prison, unless you're tunneling out, in which case small would be a plus, only Aubrey wouldn't have the nerve to try a stunt like that.

As far as girlfriends go, Aubrey has never actually had one, although he's slept with a few women he didn't have to pay. These freebies involved late nights in bars about to close, lots of beer, and women who'd just been dumped by taller men. There's one girl he's going to look up when he gets out, though, a checkout clerk at the SaveMart where Aubrey buys his weekly sack of groceries. The tag on her polo shirt says "Cheri"—the name itself full of curves and promise. A person might think she's plain unless they really looked, like Aubrey has. Then they'd notice her green eyes flecked with gold and the happy swing of her ponytail as she works. Cheri doesn't wear a wedding ring and always says "How's it going?" like she actually cares. Aubrey would never set her house on fire, even if he asked her out and she said no.

According to his World Wildlife Federation calendar, it's exactly three weeks until Aubrey's release. His sentence fairly flew by this time, what with working in the prison's blue jean business, acrylic painting classes, and Cheri to dream about. Aubrey thinks it's a good omen that his sentence began in January (polar bears), and is up in June (antelope), leaving him the best half of the year to get things right.

Marlene glares at her son through the smudged Plexiglas wall that divides visitor from visited. It blurs her a little, makes the blond wig less wiggy, melting edges off her angles. "You can stay with me for a month, two tops. No drugs, no booze, no girls, no you-know-what."

Aubrey grins at Marlene. "No, what?"

"FYI mister, there's nothing funny about riding a stinking bus full of crack whores up here to visit someone who doesn't have sense enough to pound sand in a rat hole."

This is one of Marlene's favorite sayings, which Aubrey has never understood, having seen a rat, and sand, but never a rat hole, and how would you pound sand in a hole anyway? Doesn't sound so smart to him. "I already talked to my P.O. She says the lumber mill's hiring clean-up crew and they pay seven bucks an hour to start."

Marlene stares at her son, his face aglow like it's Christmas morning and Santa just delivered a pony. She sighs. Mill plus wood plus arsonist? Frigging parole officer knows full well they'd never let her son within a mile of that tinderbox. There he sits in that godawful orange jumpsuit, which is definitely not his color, beside himself over a dead-end job he won't even get. Too dumb to know that nothing changes and if anything, you only become more of what you already are. She digs up a hopeful expression anyway, for his sake. Christ, this place makes her thirsty.

Twenty-one days later, when Marlene picks up Aubrey, he's wearing the same outfit he was arrested in: blue jeans, Planet Hollywood sweatshirt, and his special boots with the lifts that make him five foot four. All smiles, loaded down with a stack of cheery paintings featuring flowers and unicorns, you'd never guess he's torched his parents' garage, three houses, a trailer, an acre of forest, and a twelve-story warehouse in another state they could never prove. It's a bonafide miracle that nobody's been hurt or killed in one of his fires, but Aubrey's had a certain amount of luck when it comes to crime, explaining perhaps why he has yet to learn his lesson.

And sure enough, against all odds, Aubrey's cellblock

daydreams begin to come true. Despite his incendiary past, the mill agrees to hire him. Marlene suspects the boss is some born-again type, or that he torched a few anthills himself, back when. Aubrey hits the ground running on the graveyard shift, driving around importantly in a glorified golf cart that he loads with lumber scraps.

Soon he has enough cash saved to rent a room over a co-worker's garage with a microwave oven, a tiny fridge, and his own shower. Marlene whips him up some Chinese red curtains and a matching bedspread on her sewing machine, then throws in a fuzzy, fake-fur rug from Target to make the bachelor pad complete. Aubrey spends a whole week deciding where to hang his best unicorn painting, finally choosing a spot over the bed where it can do double duty—hiding a water stain and working its unicornian magic while he sleeps.

Five or six times, he finds himself poised outside the doors of SaveMart, only to lose his nerve and bolt for the parking lot, hoping Cheri didn't see him. But one sunny morning, he tears a new page off his calendar (chimpanzees) and knows that today is the day. He spruces up with a shave, a splash of Aqua Velva, and a clean T-shirt without any writing on it. There's no reason he couldn't wear his Save the Whales or even Planet Hollywood. But the outside world is so crammed with choices that, sometimes, all the deciding makes Aubrey feel like his head will explode. Thankfully he has the rules of prison life to fall back on. They can really help simplify things, like *Department of Corrections Article 36. No T-shirts with slogans or writing of any kind.*

Aubrey wheels his loaded cart up to Cheri's register, falling in behind an old lady who takes forever to dig out one dollar and twenty-six pennies from her suitcase of a purse. Cheri, wonderful person that she is, waits patiently for the old lady, never once rolling her eyes like your typical checkout-jockey. As Cheri drags Aubrey's half gallon of two percent milk across the scanner, she looks up and realizes it's that cute little guy she hasn't seen in forever. "Hey there! How's it going?"

Aubrey freezes. Panic floods in, murky waters rising over his head as clever lines rehearsed for months bob aimlessly in the swell.

Cheri senses his distress and decides to bail him out. He's really not bad, in a short, uncertain way. She grabs a jumbo box of Frosted Flakes, then its twin. "Two for one. That's a smoking deal."

Aubrey blurts out, "Sometimes, I eat 'em for dinner." His hands clamp into fists, itching to punch his stupid self in his stupid mouth.

Cheri just smiles. "Me too. Most nights, it's all I want after eight hours of this. You wouldn't believe what some people eat. There's one guy who, seriously, I think he lives on bacon and marshmallows."

Determined to keep the conversation going, Aubrey looks around for inspiration and finds nothing but a photo of massively pregnant Britney Spears on the cover of *Teen People* magazine. He realizes he's on his own here. If Cheri turns him down, he can always start shopping at the Pick 'n' Pay. "I've only got a microwave," Aubrey says. Crap! Why did he just admit that? She'll think he's some loser living over a garage. "So I eat out a lot."

Cheri cuts her eyes at him, not missing a beat in her scanning and bagging ballet. She taps a final button on the register. "Thirty-three fifty."

Aubrey waits for his receipt to unfurl, not sure how much more of this he can take before he drops dead from a heart attack. "Umm, if you ever want to grab a bite. After work or something." There's a definite squeak on the end of "something." God dang it.

Cheri hands Aubrey his receipt, glancing over her shoulder to be sure her supervisor isn't lurking around. "Thursdays are good."

No woman in his recollection has ever accepted a date from him this quick, drunk or sober. "Well," he says, stunned, "okay then."

Cheri scribbles something on a piece of paper and hands it over. He's about to say, "My name's Aubrey," but she gives him a little wave and turns to greet her next customer. Aubrey beats feet out of there, astounded by what just happened. As the glass doors slide open, he checks his reflection—pretty much the same old Aubrey, although the arms do have a nice cut from pumping iron in the prison gym. Nah, he just saw better arms on two bag boys and the produce guy. His heart sinks, then he checks the slip of paper in his hand. "Cheri, 606-3476," the "i" dotted with a tiny perfect circle. A job, an apartment, and now a date? Is it possible that his luck, which has always burned bright with his fires, but nothing else, has finally changed? The last time he flipped open a lighter was over a year ago, and since he's been out, he hasn't even bought one, or touched a book of matches.

It takes everything he's got, but Aubrey manages to wait one whole day before calling Cheri. They agree to meet at a real restaurant called the Rocking Horse Inn. Aubrey's seen it advertised on TV. It's the kind of place you'd take a prom date, if you'd ever had one. Never too late, thinks Aubrey as he irons his new khaki pants and shirt and the tie with miniature whales on it that the girl in the store had to show him how to knot.

Palms sweating, Aubrey steps cautiously into the bar at the Rocking Horse. The place is crowded with couples drinking cocktails and chatting over jazzy music, but no Cheri. He should've known. Then someone taps him on the shoulder, he turns, and there she is, in a silky dress that stops just above her tanned, bare knees. "Look at you," Cheri beams, lightly touching Aubrey's tie, close enough that he can smell her skin, her hair. His penis jump to life and he hopes to God she can't see his erection. But Cheri saves the day with a visit to the ladies' room.

She hands him her wrap as she steps away which he gladly takes, holding it over his crotch. Aubrey uses the minutes waiting for Cheri to review his numerous flaws, and by the time she returns, the erection has wilted away.

Settled at last into a discreet velvet booth, they order drinks—the house white wine for her, red for him. Aubrey can't recall ever in his life ordering a glass of wine, but beer seems too low-class, a cocktail too complicated. Soon, over roast chicken and scalloped potatoes, Cheri is chatting up a storm about her diabetic cat, the Oprah Book of the Month selection, and other girlish topics.

Like many ex-cons, Aubrey is primarily a listener, ever vigilant about the holes eaten into his life story by so much time spent behind bars. These holes must be patched with detailed lies involving careful attention to popular culture and world events, a task so exhausting that Aubrey mostly avoids people, who in turn, tend to ignore him. Yet, somehow, here he is, sharing a candlelit table with a real girl on a genuine date. Buoyed by her enthusiasm, as if he were a normal person and not a pathologically shy arsonist, Aubrey actually manages to share a few thoughts—mostly tidbits memorized from his wildlife calendar, such as how fast an antelope can run, or the family bonds of elephants.

Cheri listens, attentive to this man who clearly loves animals, impressed that he cares about such things. He even put on a tie for her (how cute are those whales), which she is certain no date since high school has ever bothered to do.

When the waiter arrives with the dessert menu, it's another first for Aubrey. An entire menu devoted to dessert! He insists Cheri order for both of them. She whispers to the waiter, who nods approvingly, then disappears, returning shortly with what looks like ordinary cherries and vanilla ice cream. Then the waiter pours a dramatic waterfall of brandy over the dish, flicks a lighter and with a whoosh, sets it blazing.

Cheri claps, delighted. Aubrey stares at the flaming cherries, at Cheri's wondrous face, as his worlds collide in a moment of terrible, breathless perfection. Cheri dips her spoon into the dish, reaches across the table, and feeds him a mouthful of scorching sweetness and heat. Her fingers brush his cheek and Aubrey's heart rips into two bloody halves as he realizes this is it, the best it will ever be. Looking down, he sees the fire already fizzling out, cherries bleeding into a puddle of melting ice cream.

Aubrey excuses himself and heads for the men's room. After five minutes, Cheri glances at her watch. After ten, she looks worriedly toward the men's room, wondering if Aubrey might be sick. At last the waiter appears with the check on a gleaming lacquer tray. "Paid by the gentleman," he says softly, sensing Cheri's dismay. A moment later, the waiter returns with a cup of steaming black espresso and a plate of chocolate truffles. "Compliments of the house."

Cheri thanks him and takes a sip of the bitter coffee she doesn't want. As if everything is fine, as though the abrupt and secretive departure of the quiet little man is no big deal, but just the way it goes when a gal is dating Superman and somewhere, disaster strikes.

At the 24-Hour Quick Stop, a sleepy clerk slides a pack of Kools across the counter. Aubrey takes the cigarettes, his hand hovering over the matchbooks beside the register. The clerk yawns, eager to be rid of his only customer. "They're free, dude. Knock yourself out." Aubrey grabs one matchbook and leaves, sweat staining his fine new shirt.

A block away, on a street lined with warehouses and weed-choked vacant lots, he tosses the cigarette pack in the gutter. He doesn't smoke, never has. Holding the matches to his nose, Aubrey breathes in the sharp sulfur smell. Overhead, the late-summer moon hangs heavy, a monstrous yellow slice, and the night air is still and dry.

Tidal

Matthew Robinson

"I MISS THE COMFORT in being sad," I say, quoting Cobain.

You smile, I think because you think I mean I'm happy—
that you make me happy. But happy and sad are a false dichot-
omy. You've distracted me out of sadness, but now I'm stuck
with the anxiety of expectations. So, fuck.

You're driving us to the coast. It's raining. I'm carsick. My
hand is in your hand, but I'd rather you had both hands on
the wheel. My palm feels clammy against yours. You stroke my
thumb and it's tender and a little sticky. I think the sticky part
is me so I pull away.

"What's wrong?" you say.

"Nothing," I say. "My arm's asleep." Some part of me is
always asleep—or worse.

An hour later we are standing on the shore. The rain has
dissipated and the sun has almost burned away the clouds.
You take my hand, the one that isn't carrying my shoes, and we
walk calf-deep into the breakers. The water is warmer than the
air, something about Japanese currents, you say. You pull me
to you. We kiss. There's salt on our lips from the sea mist and

from being human.

I start to cry.

You don't say anything, you just push harder, into me. Our faces are wet and my breath catches. I drop my shoes and take hold of your sleeve, but I don't know if I should push or pull. You are pulling with your hands and pushing with your mouth.

I stop crying. We stop kissing. I release your sleeve, but keep one hand clasped with yours. I look for my shoes, but they're gone.

"Shit," I say.

"What?" you say.

"I lost my shoes."

"Oh."

"Also, I'm sorry for crying. It's weird, I know."

Your hand squeezes mine and relaxes. You slip off your shoes by stepping on each heel, nudge them with your toe, and we watch the tide pull them away and under. It's beautiful how they go.

"There, now you haven't lost anything," you say.

In the car we smell like the ocean. Our feet are bare and the rain has returned. You are driving. I am not sad. Maybe this is happy. I don't know. It is comfortable though.

I rub my hands together and feel the grit of sand. I wipe them on my pants. I want to take your hand but am afraid the clammy feel will return. So I unbuckle and lift the armrest, I lie across the seats and put my head in your lap. I close my eyes. Twice on the drive I cry. Quietly. You lay a hand on my neck, cold against my heat.

Surely

Scott Sparling

RED TOENAILS, BLACK GRUNGE. That's what I see, looking down in the shower. The black stuff grows in the corners where the tile is cracked and in the places where I don't clean. In my old life, I would have swooped in with grunge-poison, something lemon-scented and lethal, but I'm taking a live-and-let-spread attitude about shower mold these days. About a lot of things, actually.

So yeah, it's Fungus Gone Wild near the shower drain. Feel free to mark that down against me if you're keeping score, and I know you are.

While mold doesn't bug me, my toenails do. I'm tired of red. I want to go purple, but I'll have to check on that. One-Legged God is in town tonight, playing that club that was Annie's favorite. *A one-legged god is a pretty good god*—I love that song. I can see myself at the club in my striped purple top with beaded cuffs, skater skirt, open-toed slings. The short and flippy look with an undercurrent of hot. Except that's how Annie used to dress, and believe me, I'm past all that. I'm much more urban scruffy now. White jersey, khaki tee, torn jeans. I'll have to check on that too.

I pee on the grunge-mold, wondering if girl urine is toxic or life-giving to the crud colony. Only time will tell. The water is yellow for a bit, then clears. Right after that, the shower turns cold, so the last part is stinging. The icy water feels good, and I like the way my body looks when I get out, my skin all goose-bumpy and tight in the soft sun coming through the frosted window. My crappy apartment doesn't seem so rat-ass in that light. I dry off, wrap up in a towel, and take my clean new bod to the living room so I can check in with Charles.

There's a ritual to this, not to be messed with: laptop on the floor, along with the quilt that used to be Granny's so I won't kill my knees. Thanks, Granny, and also, sorry Granny—you might want to avert your eyes if that's an option in Little Old Lady Afterlife where you surely must be, unless you're just dead.

Next to the laptop: a bowl, an onion, a knife. For clothes, the hospital gown Annie stole. The gown is paper thin and robin's egg blue. When I was a kid I saw a robin's egg at school. Someone brought it in. It was pretty to look at, but sad to think about the robin inside that was never going to hatch, and I started to cry. Not the best idea, showing weakness in third grade. Kids are humiliation experts, masters at it. Thanks for the lesson, Mrs. Rasch, boys, girls, I owe you. I lose the towel and tie the gown behind my neck, leaving the rest open for easy access, though there's no one else here. I know this wickedness well.

On elbows and knees, I crawl into the glow of the laptop until my fingers reach the keys. The message I type is a single word, one we all know but rarely say: "Master?"

I like it how some people rack up a whole lifetime of labor and never speak that truthful word. Maybe you're one of them—the people who are quick to put me down, even as they trudge off to work, half-asleep, to serve some soul-devouring, money-loving, nice-on-the-outside boss getting rich on your labor. Me, I drop the pretense and just get on my knees. I crawl like one of the creatures we all once were, defenses down, and it scares me but also makes me feel alive. Sometimes it turns me on, but mostly what it does is empty me out. For me, serving Master Charles scours out the crud until there's nothing left.

SINCE CHARLES CAME INTO my life, I've learned thirteen one-word commands, including *bara*, *nadu*, and *sula*, and a lot of other weird stuff, including how to be strong by seeming weak. And the thing is, I've never even met him. That's what most people don't get, or wouldn't get if I told anyone about Master Charles, which mostly I don't.

Another thing I've learned is that most men you meet online are dumb as stones. See also: lonely, insecure, dull, and desperate for love. They all want you to phone them, or meet them somewhere, and they beg beg beg you to send a pic. You'd think their lives depended on it. This one guy, he pings me all dominant and harsh, orders me to stand in front of my window in nothing but my conductor's hat. Fine. I'm all aboard with that. But when I won't send a pic, he goes, *How do I know you really did it?*

Listen, I want to tell him. I get off on obeying. If I don't obey, I don't get off. So why would I waste my time pretending to obey, since that totally wouldn't get me off? But I didn't bother taking him to school. I knew by his question he wasn't for me.

Then there's *Are you really a woman?* Gotta love that. Remember when they told you there's no such thing as a stupid question? They lied. I mean, what am I supposed to say? My screen name is Surely, my profile says female, my avatar is Betty Boop with a ball gag. Yes, I'm a woman.

Some geniuses believe they can divine my gender with nothing but their brilliant line of questioning. Like they're the internet's Sherlock Holmes of Sex, except they're not. This one guy goes, *You have thirty seconds to name five kinds of shoes.*

I shot him back like zap. *Peep-toes, slingbacks, pumps, wedges, mules, and big humping ugly combat boots, which is what I'm wearing right now.* Then I pinged him *Good-bye dork and have a nice chastity.* I wanted him to know that I've got more shoe intel in my little finger than he'll have in his entire pointless life, and also, note to losers, I have no use for would-be doms with trust issues.

But it's the picture-whining that makes me want to retch. You know, pose like this or that to prove you're real. Right. Like I'm sending you a picture of me with my thumb up my butt because you're such a big powerful master and also, you're terrified that you might be doing cyber with a guy. But guess what, Jackson? I'm not dropping for a dominant who's insecure. I got enough insecurities of my own.

That's what drew me to Master Charles. He got me right away. He's like, *It's not about sex*, which is totally true. It's not about sex at all. Any two idiots can get together and go at it. You only had to be Annie to know that.

THE BOWL, THE KNIFE, and the onion are to make tears fall on the keyboard. Would you have thought of that? Be honest. Probably not, right? That's why I love Master Charles. He's studied this, taken the time to understand what it means to let go of yourself. I hit erase when I met Master Charles and the old me went away, everything, including all the grunge in those places I could never reach. I changed my name. I threw out Annie's clothes. I started over. Charles said tears are part of the process. Hence the onion. A lot of people use drugs to get rid of the past. The world's more respectable types simply make a lifestyle out of repression. But that doesn't empty you out. It just covers over the mess.

While we're being honest, let me just say that I know you think you're better than me. More mature, more normal. Congratulations on your healthy, wholesome lifestyle, your fulfilling relationships, and your enormous self-esteem. Perhaps you'd like to help me, or better yet, judge me. Yes, I'm being sarcastic, duh.

And mostly truthful. By which I mean more truthful than most.

THINGS I'VE DONE FOR Master Charles: Tried on collars at PetSmart. Asked the cute librarian for books on fellatio. Handcuffed myself to the sink in the men's room of the Air Hole. Crawled through Baker's Park in the rain, naked. Given myself an orgasm on the 36 during rush hour. Gone to the drive-through in a T-shirt that said *Do Me Now, Ask Me How*. Shown my breasts in Quadrants One through Four.

Most of all, I've shown the thing that's never supposed to be shown in daylight, and by that I mean desire. Master Charles is my master. He makes me want and want and want.

THE WORLD IS FULL of people who are afraid to let go. Charles told me that on day one. Even in the middle of some epic screw-up, most people just keep plowing ahead, nose to the grind-stone, making everything worse. Not me. I met Charles and hit the restart button. Respawned myself, he would say. My name, for example—it always sounded so old to me, but not cool retro old, just embarrassing old. So now when I meet someone, I just tell them how it's spelled and everything's fine. Surely you jest, they say. I get that a lot.

IN THE LIVING ROOM, on hands and knees, tears dropping. My blue gown falling open. How long I'll wait, I don't know. It's all part of the process.

They don't actually care if you take the hospital gown when you leave, FYI. It's not really stealing, so you can't blame Annie for that. Just clarifying.

Finally Master Charles pings me, gives me permission to

hear One-Legged God at the Air Hole as long as I use the tape.

I've done this before and I know the drill. There's a Sharpie in the kitchen, so I sit at the table, tear off some masking tape, and start printing the four-word message in big black letters.

When I'm done, I stick the tape across my belly. Below the navel, above the landing strip. Right where they cut you open, where the scar is, if you have a C-section. I know that because Annie had one, and she didn't even get to keep the baby.

The message on the tape says *Property of Master Charles.* Big and proud.

In case you haven't tried—duh—it's nearly impossible to print something right side up on your own stomach, specially if you need it to be legible in some dark club. That's why the tape. More proof that Master Charles knows what he's doing.

What it says is true and I'm not ashamed of it. I used to sleep around. Now I don't. It's not allowed. Before you start clucking, let me just point out that your wedding ring says exactly the same thing, but more whorishly, since it's worth enough to be considered payment, while masking tape is just tape. So go ahead and shame me, but remember: The people who judge me most harshly are the ones who are best at lying to themselves.

Just like your wedding ring, the tape keeps me safe. It lets other men know that they can drool 'til kingdom come, but I won't be going home with them. And I certainly won't be sleeping with them.

But check it: I'm not an idiot. The tape is also Master Charles' way of being selfish. Say he's got me slurping Smirnoff from the dog dish at some party and a good-looking guy starts a game of fetch. What if we decide to hook up that night? Maybe I wouldn't be so keen about having Master Charles as my master after that.

So the tape is MC's way of protecting his investment. Those were his exact words—*protecting my investment.* Since he's never given me a cent, I know he meant his emotional investment. Honesty is a very important part of our relationship.

THE THING ABOUT STARTING over is this: everyone should do it at least once. You, for example, with those chip-and-dent values you claim to live by, until you realize you don't. Wouldn't you like to start fresh? Give yourself a second chance? But you won't, will you, not unless you're really in a tailspin, and you don't have any other choice. And even then, you'll try to talk yourself out of it.

WHEN I FIRST CHOSE Master Charles as my master, I had some good long talks. They all started with pity, pity, pity, and poor you for having such low self-esteem, and don't you know you deserve better and blah, blah, blah. Those were Annie's values, and they pissed me off.

Hey sister, I said. You act like you're so free, but that's the last thing you are. You're living in this little channel with two big boards on either side of you, and you can only go where the channel takes you and only do what you're supposed to do, and the sad part is, you don't even know it.

But old Annie was back in my face with her pre-programmed rationalization, standard equipment on most models: All that proves is that I have values, she said, and I follow them. Why shouldn't I? They're my values. I'm the one who chose them.

I was at Hall of Burgers eating fries at the time, dipping each one in ketchup, eating the red part, smearing the stub end again. I'm not allowed to eat fries anymore. Master Charles says they're bad for my complexion. Not that he's ever seen me, but check it, we're honest with each other.

Get real, Annie, I said. Way before you were born, some shitheads who were probably ashamed of their own farts propagated a whole bunch of rules about your body, what you can show, what you can't show, what you're allowed to say, what you have to wear, and what you can touch and not touch. There's a rule for everything and they call it being *nice*. And who decides what's nice and what isn't? Not you, that's for damn sure.

Not true, she said. And even if it was, it was no reason to crawl around like a perv for some fake-o internet guy. Show some self-control, girl.

That did it.

Really? I said. You think you're in control? Don't make me laugh. You aren't calling the shots any more than I am. You're doing exactly what other people tell you to do, every day, just like me. So don't you dare call me a perv. You let them tell you that you couldn't keep your own baby, for godsakes. Christ, Annie, you're a bigger sub than I am. Maybe I'm a perv, but you're the one who gave away your little girl.

I shouldn't have said that last part. I felt bad about it and I promised I would never try to guilt trip anybody again. Ever.

Sometimes, you just have to give yourself a good talking to.

ANYWAY, THAT'S ALL IN the past. Guilt is a feeling I never get with Master Charles.

This is how it works: If all on my own I decide to answer the door in my undies and rub up against the pizza guy, I'll feel like shit afterwards, because according to the world, rubbing up against the pizza guy is wrong.

But if Master Charles orders me to do it, different story. I don't feel guilty. I just feel brave, or daring, or turned on. Sure, I'm not following the world's rules. But I'm not the one responsible for breaking them either. I'm just a body put in motion by Master Charles. That's what he calls it. So if the idea of me stripping at the industrial park pisses you off, get pissed at Master Charles, because it's his idea. I'm just the one feeling the sun on my skin.

I'm the body, he's the mind, see? And guess what? All the bad stuff's in the mind.

I LIVED IN MY head once. I didn't like it very much. We're talking Pre-Charles here. Gorrf, my sometimes boyfriend back then, was a supposedly hotshot guitar player because who isn't? But his band was actually halfway decent, which only means they sucked fractionally less than a lot of bands and lasted a day or two longer before going down the drain.

Back in prehistoric one-and-a-half years ago, Gorrf had two big dreams. To build a practice space for his band behind a rental house his dad owned, and to get inside my pants.

Gorrf was the kind of dude who planned his work and worked his plan. Despite the crazy name.

When the practice space was done, he took me over there. Behold, he said, as we stepped inside. Gorrf's Enchanted Musical Paradise and Private Love Nest.

To me it was just an enlarged playhouse, but I didn't say so. What had him all jacked up was the shape.

The walls aren't parallel! he proclaimed. Like that was a marvel to be pondered at great length. To me it sounded like a flaw. Like, what else would you expect if you gave Gorrf a hammer and let him loose.

So what, I said. I didn't care about the walls. I was checking out the futon, covered with a furry throw thing from the Maximum-Cheese aisle of the closest man-cave store. The futon was the reason he'd driven me over there, so naturally we had to pretend it wasn't.

Gorrf was still twirling and gaping at the purposely fucked-up walls.

It's so the sound waves can't bounce around and run into each other and get all smashed up, he said. He stroked the straw-colored beard that made him look like a loser in the Confederate Army, or like the model for a whisk broom. There was lust in the way he tugged it. Non-parallel walls are essential for making beautiful music, he said.

I looked back and forth a bunch of times but couldn't see it.

Finally I just took his word that the angles were off. Like I said, I'd have been more surprised if they weren't.

The walls inside my head, on the other hand, formed a perfect square. Everything I thought echoed and ricocheted, coming back at me in negative angles. Will Gorrf stop seeing Sandy if I conquer my resistance and finally do it with him? Or maybe if I don't sleep with him, he'll respect me more and finally see Sandy as the Licensed and Bonded Slut-o-matic that she is. Sex or no sex? Caution or full speed ahead? Condom or trust Gorrf? Now or never?

It's no wonder I barely enjoyed sex with all those neurons colliding, the nonstop crash and burn. Before I discovered Charles, there was never any way to have a simple, pure thought about anything.

Honestly, I don't know how you do it, all you regular folks, you square-thinkers you. Getting up every morning and hitting your marks with a Left, Right, Left, Right, March! Don't you get tired of being wrong all the time?

Also, why would anyone sleep with a dork named Gorrf?

PERMISSION TO ATTEND THE One-Legged God show does not come without a price. In return for granting my request, MC pings me saying he wants a Third Quadrant nipple slip. To remind me that I'm his and that nothing is free.

Q3 is Accidental Exposure with Discovery and Arousal. It's the hardest because you have to be a good actress and get all surprised when your tit pops out, like the whole thing is news to you. But you're not embarrassed. That's Q2—Accidental with Discovery and Embarrassment. In Q3, the wardrobe malfunction turns you on and you don't try to hide it.

I ping MC back. Right or left? He says *Left, six seconds*.

That's how much of a control freak he is. Six, not five. Six seconds is an eternity, but I can do it. I'll have to wear something different, though. You can't fall out of a T-shirt/jersey combo.

Plus Master Charles wants it at the Hall of Burgers. A little teat for the counter guy, spends half his life in a paper hat, deserves a break today. Fair enough. Hall of Burgers is in the opposite direction from the Air Hole, and I was hoping to get this done with one bus ride. But que sera sera, like they say, which is Latin for what the fuck.

ARE ZOOS IMMORAL? THAT T-shirt you're wearing, was it made in Cambodia? How many fossil fuels got burned so you could import your earth-friendly bamboo floor from Timbukwherever? Is it worth having people starve so we can make ethanol? Do you care who the drones kill? Are you really going to deduct that so-called business dinner? How is that CD you burned not exactly like stealing? Can you get rich without ripping someone off?

In other words, Jack, don't you have better things to worry about besides shaking your bony finger at me? What do you have against my nipples? Why don't you just go fuck yourself? Oh, I know. Because you're too big a prude.

I'M AT HALL OF BURGERS by seven in my tube top, ordering a Double Whammy meal and a Coke, and the counter guy is showing no interest in my tits. He's kind of a young pup, dark-framed glasses, hair-swoop like he gelled and immediately got caught in a very stiff nor'wester, and a polite/earnest voice as he inquires after my appetite needs. I'm a hundred percent sure he doesn't have a girlfriend. He hasn't even looked at my chest, but he will.

I watch as the pup grabs my DW from the window. He puts it in a basket with the rest of my order, furnishes me with a soda cup and tray. I hand him a ten, and while he's making change I pull the left side of my top down very low. We're not at tits-a-poppin' stage yet, but it won't take much.

My plan is to drop the change when he gives it to me. I'll

kneel down to get it, reach up to the counter, arch my back, and introduce him to my left mammary and its luscious tip. Hello, World, and pardon me while I supercharge every single air molecule in Hall of Burgers with a few square inches of flesh that I see every day. Maybe a surreptitious tug will be needed to start the show, and if so no prob. I'm not exactly sure how I'll pass the six seconds, but I'll think of something. Eye contact and a slow smile, etc., etc. If I'd worn the cami, I could go all come hither while adjusting the strap. Adding to the air of arousal. Note for next time.

Counter pup seems to be math challenged, though, because it's taking a while to get my change, potentially introducing nervousness on my part. I take a breath. The way I see it, I'm getting a Double Whammy, he's getting a hard-on. Thinking about it that way makes it easier, like I'm doing some good in the world.

Before all this can happen, another customer walks right up behind me, complicating things. I do a quick peripheral scan, hoping it's not an Inappropriate Person, like my dead granny or a youngster. Instead, I see a good-looking guy, my age, untended hair that easily attains perfect-mess status, and the kind of crooked smile that always turns me on. All good things in and of themselves, but the stunner is how this guy is dressed. Jeans and a One-Legged God T-shirt.

The shirt sends me into brain freeze for a second or two, tripping internal alarms like when an airplane stalls. By the time I recover, my change has been delivered and is already in my purse. So there's that. Young pup asks earnestly if there's anything else I want. A do-over maybe? But I don't say it. I pull my tube top up normal and retreat with my tray, left nip unslipped.

The thing is, One-Legged God is not a very popular band. I didn't even know they had T-shirts.

As I leave the line, cool guy gives me a quick hey. I hey him right back. Eventually he procures a drink and a Whammy and sits a couple tables over from me. The place is empty but for us, two young music lovers with fast-food appetites, so I call over to him about the shirt. He looks at it, as if he's surprised to find it on his chest. Then he tells me he's the drummer.

This I doubt, because the drummer is blond, but he says, no, the old drummer got arrested and he's the man now, but this is only his second gig, he doesn't even know all the songs.

Well, then, I think. My heart's going a little fast, faster than it was when I was about to thrill the pup. I pick up my food and join him at his table.

I probably know the songs better than you do, I tell him. He cops to that. We talk about the set list, and he tells me about his cymbals and the type of sticks he likes, and as we talk he offers me some of his fries.

I say no thanks. Master Charles and all. Even though Hall of Burgers has the best fries in the world.

His name is Rob. I tell him my name is Surely. He dips a fry into ketchup and puts it in his mouth. And then again, and one more after that. Seeing this warms something in me that hasn't been warm in a while and I realize I've been giving up a lot. Not just fries but everything. Like *everything*. My name. My baby.

Yeah, like you don't have any secrets. Like you haven't made any huge-ass mistakes and felt like you didn't deserve to crawl this earth. Besides, I told you *mostly* truthful from the start.

Freaking Gorrf. Freaking the whole judgmental world.

So that's that. I have some fries because they smell great and to hell with Master Charles, but I'm trembling as I eat.

Afterwards I feel better. Afterwards Rob asks me if I want a ride to the Air Hole. Afterwards I say, sure, absolutely, man. Without a doubt.

We arrive way early, so I get to stand around and watch them set up. In the light I can see how dingy the place is, the flat black paint all scuffed, silver duct tape holding wires and shit together. I've been to the Air Hole dozens of times, but never seen any of this stuff. It's disillusioning, and also eye-opening. As in open your eyes, Shirley Ann, see the real world.

Then the music starts and it's better than ever. Clearly, the old drummer sucked big time. Why hadn't I ever noticed that? Rob's sticks fly and hover, like Bruce Lee with stop motion, and the crookedy smile says that he's as amazed as anyone. I guess my heart must still be a little bit open, because some of the songs actually choke me up a bit, which is both weird and embarrassing. The Air Hole is made for shouting, not sobbing.

After the encore, the band disappears. I'm about to say que sera when Rob hops out and finds me milling by the door. The guys are debriefing slash getting high, he explains, but he plans to boogie and can I wait by his car, which is something I'm quite qualified and eager to do. He splits again, and I walk to his ride where I stand guard against the driver's side door. I'm not exactly sure what I'm waiting for, but the air feels good after the heat of the club.

Then Rob comes and we're driving fast, the way he drums, one hand spinning the wheel, foot on the pedals, this way, that way, I'm a little bit lost. Maybe he's driving me back to the Hall of Burgers, maybe somewhere else. I don't ask because I don't care. We're moving forward into the night and the fresh wind makes me feel new. I'm still buzzed, high on the show, and I think it's the music that's changed things, made me braver, like the best music can.

I shout at him over the wind and tell him my real name.

Surely you jest, comes the answer.

When we pull up to a light, he gives me a sideways look and the crookedy smile, and I tell him that a one-legged god is still a pretty good god.

Crazy girl, he says.

The way he says it makes me both happy and a little afraid.

I suck in my stomach, slip my hand under my belt, and pull the tape off the scar on my belly.

The light turns green and we're driving again.

Yeah, I say to him. That's me. Crazy girl.

The Pink on Her Toenails

Jackie Shannon Hollis

I ALWAYS THOUGHT I'D take Ashley dancing at Frisco's. When she got old enough to get into bars, I'd take her there and it would be legit and I'd have known her long enough that it wouldn't be me scammin' on my friend's sister. I've known Josh three years and, by way of him, I've known Ashley that long too. Something about Ashley made me want to dance with her, so I figured sometime we'd be going to Frisco's together. Me and Ashley. And we'd dance and see how that worked and then go from there.

It's not like there aren't other girls. There are. I usually go dancing at Frisco's alone but, sometimes, I find a girl there. Maybe even take her home. I hit the place around ten, ten thirty. Take an hour to sip up a few drinks, get a little loose, scope out the floor. Get a feel for the music. See who the girls are, what guys are already moving in on what girls. How the girls are taking it.

It's crazy how, if a bunch of girls are dancing together and some wrong guy starts moving in on one of them, they just swallow her into their bunch so the guy can't get to her. They do it like they're just dancing, but they're not, they're protecting one of their own. They do it in a pretty way, like those gazelles you see on the animal channel—except those animals run when there's danger. These girls, they just keep dancing.

Ashley's the kind of girl who'd like to go out dancing. I've seen her in her bedroom, moving to some poppy girl music. She can move. The bathroom at Josh's house is right next to Ashley's bedroom and Ashley leaves her door open a little. Well, it's hard not to look. I saw her there—she just had a T-shirt and panties on. No bra under that shirt. Those legs of hers looked even longer like that. The pink on her toenails. The way she moved, just a little slower than the beat of the song, but still with the music.

Ashley isn't why I'm friends with Josh, but she's a good reason for me to be the one who offers to drive when Josh and I go out for a night. That way I can hang out at Josh's house for awhile, maybe see Ashley. Josh is always running late and I always get there early. For sure Josh's dad will sit on the sofa and talk to me.

Mr. Jefferies is all right. He's kind of messed up, his wife leaving and all. She left the year Josh graduated high school, before I ever met Josh. Now she's living with a woman, but that's all I really know because Josh doesn't say much about it. I guess he doesn't say anything at all.

Mr. Jefferies tries to talk to me like he knows what's going on in the world. He talks about the economy, about "that dipshit president who fucked things up and left before he got the blame." Says how he's never seen this kind of thing, the way the world is, and, "Frankly Aiden, I'm a little worried."

But sometimes Mr. Jefferies says more than I want to hear. One time he started talking about Josh's mom. "She's just confused," he said. Which made some sense. Then he went and told me how, the day she left, she told him she loved him but didn't love being with him. "I guess she meant sex," Mr. Jefferies said. That was a little too much for me. I excused myself to the bathroom. When I left the room, Mr. Jefferies had his elbows on his knees and his face in the open palms of his hands. He was moving his face back and forth, rubbing it hard.

When I first met Ashley, she was just fifteen and had braces and no chest to speak of. Usually there were some girls with her and they'd be silly and giggly and wouldn't stay in the room long because Josh would come in and yell at Ashley to quit bugging me. It never really fazed her. Her and her friends would just roll their eyes and cover up their bracey smiles with their hands and then go off to Ashley's room. I wasn't really into her then. I mean it was my first year of college and she was still just a little girl. But I never had a brother or sister and I kind of liked the idea. According to Josh it was a pain in the ass, having a little sister.

When Ashley turned sixteen it was like she was a different girl. She grew her hair out. Now it's straight and blond and long. She got those braces off. Her eyes are blue, but they're dark and they slant a little, so she's got this exotic thing going, even though she's got that all-American girl look too. I told her that once, that she could be a model, and Josh got all over me about it. "You don't go scammin' on your friend's sister. It messes things up."

She's eighteen now and when I come get Josh she sometimes comes out into the living room and talks for a minute or two. She always uses my name. "Hi Aiden," she says when she sees me. Her voice is soft, like a pillow. And then she'll say something like, "So what've you been up to, Aiden?" If Ashley doesn't come out to the living room, I usually end up having to use the bathroom anyway and I go slow by the door to her room. Ashley's taller than Josh, but she's got these curves that make her not gangly. They make her, well, hot.

THE REASON WE WENT back tonight to Josh's house was for the weed. Josh meant to bring it so we could smoke before we went to Calhoun's, where all the guys were meeting up. But we got to the bar and that's when Josh remembered he didn't have it with him. We went into Calhoun's anyway.

Calhoun's is nothing like Frisco's. Where Frisco's is all about the dancing and they know me there, and they give me free drinks some of the time, Calhoun's is a chain kind of place, a sports bar kind of place. It's more lit up and everywhere you look there's a TV. There's gotta be, like, fifty TVs. So when you're with people, they're never really looking at you, they're looking up above your head at basketball or football or soccer or golf or tennis or whatever the hell else is on the screen up there.

We had a few pounders and some burgers and hung with the guys. But then it was about ten and Josh says we have to leave and we might be back. This was a surprise, because Josh likes Calhoun's and he likes the guys and he likes sports and he likes to pound the pounders. But maybe he saw I really wanted to smoke some weed or maybe he was bothered because of what his dad said earlier.

His dad was going on a date with some woman he'd met online. When Josh and I were going out the door, Mr. Jefferies said, and I think it was a joke but maybe Josh didn't take it as one, "If I leave the porch light off, it means I've brought her home." And he wiggled his eyebrows and elbowed Josh in the ribs and Josh said, "Jesus, Dad. You're sick." When we were in the car I asked Josh if his dad was serious and he said of course not.

When we got back to Josh's house the porch light was on. Plus, there were a few low lights on in the front room when we got in.

I wish it would've been Mr. Jefferies and some old lady. But it was Ashley there on the big sofa. She was with this twit guy that sometimes takes her out. I've seen him a few times before, but I didn't figure it was anything serious; I was sure he'd be out of the picture by the time Ashley got to know me better. But here she was with her bare legs wrapped around him and his pasty pale ass going up and down between those beautiful legs. Her little pink toenails caught the light.

Fuck. That's all I could think and maybe even said, along with the breath that came out of me like I'd taken a punch in the gut. Even though I've never taken one, it's what I imagined. But it was Josh who surprised me even more. "Fuck sakes, Ashley." He was totally casual about it and, while Ashley and that twit were scrambling to cover up and see who was there, Josh said, "How many times I have to walk in on you 'til you realize you should take it to the bedroom. I mean, what if I was Dad?"

The twit had jumped back behind the sofa, but not fast enough for me to miss the size of his dick and the way his balls hung down. Ashley had pulled two of the big pillows from the sofa over herself. She made herself small in the corner of the sofa, sitting up and tucking her legs under her. She covered her top parts with one big pillow and her bottom parts with the other. Her hair wasn't smooth anymore and her eyes were all smeary with makeup. "Shut up, Josh," was all she said. She wouldn't even look at me.

Josh sat down on the sofa, grabbed the remote from the coffee table. He nodded at me and then at the recliner and said, "Grab a seat, maybe we can catch the last part of that game." I had no idea what game he was talking about and for sure I didn't want to sit, but Josh looked like he was staying awhile and I could either stand there by the door, looking like a total dumbass, or I could just sit down and act natural. That's what I did, even though I don't think I was too natural. I mean, always before with Ashley I'd been kind of teasing with her. But I couldn't find a joke in this shit.

Josh asked me if I wanted a beer and I said, "I guess so." Nothing like a guy who can't make up his mind. Then he said, "How about it, Ashley? Want one? Does Trevor there want one?" Ashley just kept hugging those two pillows in front of her. Her jaw went between a tremble and a clench, back and forth, and Josh didn't move.

I got up. I took my time. The beer was at the back of the fridge, behind a greasy package of lunchmeat and a leftover pot of spaghetti. I left the fridge door open while I looked for the bottle opener. There was water and noodles and soggy chips and bowls and glasses all mixed up in the sink. Smears of sauce on the counter, a knife with a gob of butter on it.

I didn't offer a beer to Ashley or the twit guy, who was still behind the sofa. He was up on his knees, resting his arms on the back of it. He was watching the game. Ashley kept saying, "Josh. God. Josh," and holding those pillows tight. Once she said my name. "Aiden." Her chin trembled again. She never even looked at the twit, which I could've taken some hope from if I hadn't seen what they'd been doing.

Josh went into his bedroom and got the weed. I stood up because, for sure, it was time to go. But Josh sat back down. So I did too. He took his time filling the pipe, took a long hit, then another. He passed the pipe to me. I put the pipe up to my mouth, pretended to take a hit, but I didn't. Last thing I needed was to get knocked on my ass by Josh's skunky weed. I was already knocked on my ass.

Josh asked Ashley and the guy if they wanted some. They did. I had to get up and hand the pipe to Ashley because she couldn't move and Josh wouldn't pass it to her. She held the top pillow with one arm and had to let go of the bottom pillow to take the pipe. The pillow sort of balanced there and then it started to tilt and I pushed it back with my hand. I didn't look at her. "Thanks, Aiden," she said.

Then we sat there even longer. Eyes on the game. No one really talking. I never really looked at her, not directly. But still, I couldn't help seeing her.

Finally, it was me that got Josh to leave. "Let's go back to Calhoun's," I said. Even though I didn't really want to go there,

I was feeling bad for Ashley and almost bad for the twit, whose knees must have been getting sore there on the floor behind the sofa. And the room wasn't all that warm.

When we got in the car Josh took out the pipe. He took three monster hits then he held the pipe out to me. "No, man," I said. He made his eyes big, like he was all shocked. "What's up with you?" he said. I shrugged. "You know. Driving and all." I turned the car on and headed back to Calhoun's.

I pulled up in the almost-empty parking lot of the Shop 'n' Go, which is where we always park because it's behind Calhoun's. Josh got right out but I sat there and stared at the lighted up windows of the store, which was usually closed that time of night. But their lights were on and people in red aprons and holding clipboards moved around in there.

Josh tapped his hand on the car window and said, "C'mon dude. Let's go in, it's cold out here."

I couldn't get it out of my mind. Ashley there on the couch, her legs, that twit guy's ass between her legs, how her eyes were closed and her head tipped back. I stayed in the car and hoped Josh would go away, forget about me, which was possible with those three monster hits he took.

But he didn't forget. He kept hitting my window with the palm of his hand and then he started pushing against the car, making it rock back and forth. One of the guys from the Shop 'n' Go, a big guy with a shaved head and baggy pants, came up to the store window and cupped his hands around his face. He stood there looking at Josh rocking the car, me sitting there letting him. Then he waved his arm and said something to the other people in the store.

I swung the car door open hard and got out. "Cut it out." I pushed Josh aside with one hand. Not hard, but hard enough to get him to stop messing with my car.

"Well c'mon then," he said. "I'm freezin' my dick off." He took a few steps backward, and punched air like he was some kind of boxer. Then he stopped. "You see the size of Trevor's balls?"

Two other people, a guy and a girl, had come up to the windows in the Shop 'n' Go. All three of them standing there, looking out at us.

I didn't want to think about Trevor's balls or his dick or Ashley's mouth, how it was partway open when we walked in on them. "I think I'm gonna go home," I said. "You can get a ride from one of the guys."

Josh stopped his boxing. He tipped his chin up and looked at me. "You aren't on some kind of skids because of my little sister, are you? I mean, shit, I told you, don't be thinking about tapping her."

I put my hands in my pockets and looked back at my car, the store, those people standing there like we were some great movie instead of just a couple lame ass guys in a parking lot.

"Don't sweat it, man." Josh light-punched my shoulder. "That Ash, she's kind of a slut that way. Go for it if you want."

Before anything like a thought happened, I punched Josh. The minute my fist hit him, I knew it could be the end of us. I also knew that even though I was taller, he was stronger. He could get a good hold on me. He could hurt me. I didn't care.

My punch landed in his gut, dead center, as if I'd really aimed. Josh wasn't ready for it. He bent over and went backward two steps. He took one big breath. Then he puked. All the beer he'd had, the burger from Calhoun's. It came out fast and he stayed bent over for it.

I looked back at the Shop 'n' Go. Those two guys and that girl were pointing and laughing. I just stood there, my arms at my sides, like Josh could hit me back if he wanted. He spit and straightened up.

I was ready for him, ready for him to charge at me, ready for him to yell. I'd let him. It felt like I'd already been hit as bad as I could be.

But he didn't. "Huh," he said. "Good shot." He shook his head, rubbed his gut. "Didn't know you had it in you." When he walked away, there wasn't anything mad in his shoulders. The way he held his head at an angle was like he was trying to figure something out, something that didn't make any sense.

Hunk

Dylan Lee

THE WOMAN WAS TIRED of guys being guys, so she drove to the movie studio to find herself a hunk.

She found her way to an abandoned back lot behind a tropical isle set that was falling apart. The Island, as they called it, had been used long ago for an action spy movie, for a sitcom about a woman who finds herself stranded with the man she said she wouldn't sleep with if he were the last man on earth, and most recently for a documentary about the Dominican Republic.

The lot was covered in a light gray and uneven asphalt, dotted with empty makeup bottles and sickly green weeds sprouting through thin, long cracks. It was where they put all of the characters whose movies were finished and forgotten, the characters who didn't get sequels. They were all wandering around, scriptless, inside the high chain-link fence. When she first arrived, the woman thought they were extras in a zombie movie.

When the woman saw him, she knew he was the one. Tall. Well dressed, like he was going to a ball. He smiled like her first boyfriend in high school. But this one had muscles.

His name was Chad, and he was the lead in a cable TV movie about a young man who was down on his luck so he went to war and jumped on a grenade to save his squad and was nursed back to health by a nurse who had sworn herself off men because she was raped by her stepfather back in Kansas but Chad opened her heart again and they fell in love while fighting off Nazis in a Warsaw bakery.

Chad and the woman who was tired of guys liked each other immediately. Chad took the woman to dinner, to the movies, and out to clubs, without showing the littlest bit of insecurity about dancing in front of other guys.

On top of his six-foot frame, Chad's head was blessed with coal black hair that was thick and always shiny, always perfect. Perfect after wearing a hat for ten hours straight. Perfect after a touch football game. Perfect after a roller-coaster ride.

Chad's cheeks were chiseled like a G.I. Joe doll's. But he never had any facial hair, even after he and the woman had spent all day together. His eyes sparkled green and often looked right into hers, getting brighter and greener as they did.

She looked up into them one night at her doorstep. "Your eyes are so beautiful, a color I've never seen before. Almost unnatural."

"I only wish they were as beautiful as yours," he said. And he said it without sarcasm, and the woman thought she heard an orchestra playing.

"Do you hear that, that beautiful music?" she asked.

"Yes. It always plays when I say beautiful words to a beautiful woman."

The woman laughed softly, opened her front door, and pulled him inside her home for the first time.

She led him to the bedroom and began unbuttoning his perfectly pressed, black oxford. She kissed his ear and whispered close, "You've respected me. You've never pushed for this. You've never told me a lie to get me in bed."

He whispered back, "It was never my line, my love."

But the woman heard only her own heavy breathing and then her moist lips pressing against soft skin covering rock-hard muscles. She was having sex with the kind of man she always thought of when she'd had sex with other men.

The woman slid open a drawer and pulled out a small, thin, square package. It crinkled when she held it up. "Would you mind?" she asked.

"We won't need contraceptives," Chad said. "I can't give or get STDs. And I can't have children."

He gently caressed her shoulder and his eyes glowed greener.

He said, "You aren't thinking about having children with me, are you, my love?"

"Of course not," she said softly. "We've only just met." On the bedside table, her eyes fixed on a book about baby names that hadn't been there before.

He said, "I hope you don't mind. I put it there for dramatic effect and to instill a greater sense of irony. Habit."

In the middle of the night, the woman woke still smiling from sex and turned to her perfect lover. He, too, was awake. His looks-even-better-with-his-clothes-off body lay naked next to her, every muscle and curve defined under the thin sheet. She said, "There's an extra toothbrush in the bathroom."

"Thank you. You're wonderful. But I don't need it."

"I thought you brushed your teeth all the time. Your breath is always so nice and fresh. And your teeth are so, well, so perfect."

Chad said, "That's how they wrote my breath. That's how they wrote my teeth."

In the morning, Chad woke up and didn't go to the bathroom.

"Never?" she asked.

"Never."

She said, "Well, that means we'll save a lot on toilet paper and water bills."

Chad looked at her as a laugh track played all around them. And he said, "You're the funniest woman I've ever met." And she knew he meant it. And he kissed her deeply.

The woman left for work, but Chad said he didn't have a job. Though every time he opened his wallet, there was cash. And his credit cards were never denied. The woman thought about quitting the PR business, but the thought of staying home all day and having sex and all the money she ever wanted scared her. She thought there would have to be a catch. So she kept going into work, but she told her boss what she really thought of him. He never fired her. He left her alone and acted a lot less like a dick.

For the first couple of days the sex was better than the woman had ever experienced. Orgasms were regular. For her.

One morning, she came out of the bathroom and sat down on the bed next to Chad. She lightly placed her hand on his muscular thigh and asked, "Are you not excited by me? Is there some sort of medical problem? It's okay. I'll still love you."

Chad only smiled and held her tightly. "Darling, you are the most fantastic lover I've ever had. But I've never had an orgasm, and I never will." He picked up his Italian leather wallet and took out a white business card with red type. "But I want you to be happy. I have the number of a friend who can help. Roc Hardon. He's still making films, and he's had lots of jobs. Such as a deliveryman, or a pool boy, or once he even was a doctor who made house calls. Would you like his card?"

The woman lifted a finger to his lips and pressed gently. His mouth stopped talking and turned up in a smile. The woman and her Chad said nothing more and she stayed home that day and they made love many times. Chad always knew what she liked. He always held her afterward. He always slept in the wet spot.

A few weeks passed, and the woman came home to find her Chad in the arms of another woman. This other woman's back was to the woman, with silky blond hair halfway down to her waist. She was shapely, with perfect curves and the designer-jeans-clad ass of a seventeen-year-old.

The woman closed the front door behind her, a sharp bang announcing her presence, and said, "I knew it."

The *other* woman twirled around, she and Chad both smiling.

Chad said, "Darling, this is my mother. I just told her about us."

Chad's mother was not seventeen, but looked only about five years older than Chad. Her smile widened, revealing perfectly straight, gleaming white teeth tucked behind red, plump lips. The lips moved and said, "I love her already," and she stepped forward, arms out for an embrace. And she really did love the woman already.

Months went by. A year. Almost two. Chad built her a boat. Chad built her a horse ranch. Chad rode like a knight in shining armor. The woman was happy. The woman was worried.

One morning, while eating homemade waffles on the porch of the cabin Chad built just steps from a lake, the woman asked, "Would you ever leave me?"

Chad took her hand in both of his. There was a dramatic backlight behind him, even though the porch light was off, and it was still dim everywhere else and full of shadows. He said, "I would never leave you. Not for the moon. Not for every star in the sky." A shooting star arced behind him right on cue.

She said, "Aren't there any perfect women from your other life, you know, before me, who don't burp or fart or drop things or burn food?"

He gently squeezed her hand tighter and softly brushed her split-ended, bed-head hair out of her eyes. "There's no one else for me. I would never, ever consider it."

She looked back up at him and said, "What if I asked you to?"

Chad leaned forward and kissed her with a kiss that she never wanted to end. And she worried more.

The woman came home late one night in a black and silver Badgley Mischka cocktail dress, put down her Gucci bag on the couch stuffed with goose feathers from Egypt, and she asked, "Who is it?"

"Hello, my love. Who is who?" he asked, sprinkling carrot shavings on the salad he was making her just the way she liked it.

"Who is the antagonist?" she said, folding her arms in front of her chest.

"I don't know," Chad said, as his hands paused in turning the pepper mill. "I don't think we have one, sweetie."

The woman took a step closer to Chad. She stared at him. "There's always an antagonist."

With a smile, he said, "Would you like it to be Roc? He's often the bad guy. Did you notice I put his card up on the refrigerator yesterday? His number is 555-anything. You just dial 555 and then any four more digits and it always reaches him."

The woman unfolded her arms and sat down on the brushed-aluminum barstool. She looked down, avoiding eye contact, trying not to fall into the trap of his sympathy, generosity, and sincerity.

"I don't want Roc Hardon . . . to be the bad guy."

"Honey, it's okay. Even when he's arrested, he just has sex with the cops. You can even be a cop. You just need to not wear a bra." He placed her salad in front of her, next to a glass of her favorite red. "What's the matter, darling? Have I done something not right?"

With two fingers on the base, the woman gently pushed the wine glass away from her. She wanted Chad to forget to put the toilet seat down. She wanted him to forget her birthday. She wanted him to stare at other women's tits. She wanted him to get sick so she could take care of him. She wanted to have children with him, children he could curse in front of.

That night, the woman and Chad made passionate love in four different rooms and on two staircases. Chad fell asleep holding the woman. But the woman could not sleep.

Straddling him, she took a round, moist makeup sponge and gently wiped it across his forehead. She looked at the path the sponge had taken, and in the dim light from the window she could see all the way through to the pillow.

Chad said, "Honey, what are you doing?" He opened his eyes, but she quickly wiped across each of them, leaving imperfect, empty sockets.

He said, "Darling . . .?"

Dramatic violin music rose in the air around them. The woman wiped the sponge across his mouth, rubbing out any chance for a flawlessly convincing argument. She erased his cheeks, his eyebrows, his ears, the waves of his rich black hair, and as the violins crescendoed, she wiped and wiped and wiped away every last perfect bit of his body.

Splinters

Lois Rosen

1.

"Honey, honest to God," Marty said. "Marble stairs."

"Marble stairs in Yonkers?" I said. "You're kidding."

"No. A spanking new building, next to the synagogue. Better yet, rent-controlled." One, two, three, he waved the ad. "*Bubeleh*, wanna take a look-see soon?"

Right away I told him, "Yes, first thing tomorrow." Then I started weeping.

"What're you getting so emotional about?" He dabbed my tears with his white hanky.

He didn't know how it was all the years above the store in those attic rooms, if you could call them that. A wood staircase we learned not to climb barefoot or splinters jabbed. Me in a narrow closet, the brothers, the big shots, in a real room, our parents squeezed in another. Walls—thin sheets of wood. Up and down that ladder-like staircase.

Marble. Had anyone in Yonkers ever seen such a staircase, wide as two people, arms open, for the queen of England lifting her royal feet to ascend and descend?

And me, climbing with him to an apartment in that palace of a building. Banisters polished smooth, up four flights to our love nest, our paradise.

2.

If only I could have traveled to the Catskills with him to some hotel like the Concord where they feed you vast platters of blintzes, steaming bowls of borsht, salty lox like no other. But after Marty's jaw cancer, him unable to eat one bite away from home, what would have been the point?

My sixteen-year-old, I dragged once, not to the Concord, the fanciest of the fancy, but to the Pinegrove Hotel in Kerhonkson, a five-day, mid-week special. So what that the comedians making the circuit came there last, and not the big names like Mel Brooks or Sid Caesar but some comic you never heard of?

July heat rose like flames to the fourth floor. "Honey," I said, "Let's get out of this frying pan of an apartment."

She grimaced at me like I was liver, tough to chew, though it's so good for the blood.

She answered, "If I have to."

Right then, I could've smacked her one. But she was a teenager. The last thing she wanted was to be roped into being my partner on the dance floor. Every other woman dancing with her husband, the complete set—a mother and a father.

3.

It's not like you get over sorrow fast, take off widow's weeds, those *shmatas,* the end. "Widow," the sign on your chest no one caresses. And every eye stares at you on the street, in the supermarket aisle, in the synagogue, at your blackish-green glow: Widow, widow, bereft, the Titanic sinking. If you had any guts, you'd throw yourself into the Hudson, or more convenient, off the fire escape rungs. Gutless wonder. *Guttenyu,* dear God, what am I to do?

The broom handle I hold to steady myself as I sweep and sweep not one crumb dropped from his mouth. Today I'd get down on my knees, gather what fell, and swallow.

Mishuga, I've become a nutcase. Maybe cook a little something, but what ingredient has his flavor, his skin, the hair up and down his arms, his sweat, his salt?

Middling

Victoria Blake

A NUMBER OF YEARS ago, I spent two weeks at my friend's property in the valleys to the north of Tucson. The property sat on five acres on the border of the desert. At the time, I considered five acres to be an estate. On my last night, Michelle—that was my friend's name—made us both beds outside on the concrete pool deck, where we slept under light sheets, looking up at what seemed on that night to be the universe's largest full moon. My memory of the trip is dominated by the dry, dry heat, which sucked the sweat directly from my skin and the nape of my neck, of the powdery feel of sunscreen, and of the cool pool lapping on the soles of my feet, and of Michelle in her big straw hat, smoking her two cigarettes a day, an old habit recently revived, because life is short, because why the hell not.

Michelle was my older friend, a previous neighbor when I was a few years out of college and living in Denver. I had just started dating Jeffery when I met her. Her kids had recently left the nest, and her husband had convinced her to downsize to the condos across the street from the apartment I rented, the first place I'd lived by myself. It is the rare person, I think, who, like

Michelle, is able to cross a thirty-year age span without fear or self-importance or separation. Her husband worked late, and Michelle would invite me over to dinner, or we would go see a movie, or, on the weekends, she would take me up to the mountain to ski. We got facials and read the same books and talked about how sex for me was different than sex for her, because I was twenty-five and figuring it out with Jeffery, and she was fifty-two and married for thirty years, and it wasn't like sex went away, but it certainly changed, and isn't that interesting. Life, she said, will keep you guessing, that's for sure. During the year I spent in Denver, I considered her to be the closest person to me, both mother and sister. She was the one who drove me to the dentist when I had my wisdom teeth out, and I was the one who made her brownies for her fifty-third birthday, which was a sad birthday for her, because she missed her kids.

After a year of living across the street from each other, Michelle and her husband moved from Colorado to Arizona. The desert, she said, would save her soul. "Save?" she said. "I meant salve. Like an ointment. Salve, not save." She made it clear that I was welcome any time.

They moved in the fall. That winter, Jeffery decided that his life was going places he didn't want me to follow—a decision he quickly regretted, and came back, flowers and chocolates in hand, correctly believing that he could wriggle his return into my heart—but during those months when Jeffery was gone and life seemed one-dimensional with no clear fix in sight, I put in all my vacation time and flew to see Michelle in her new life in the desert. She was, she has always been, a sort of model for me.

THE FIRST TIME I met Jeffery I didn't like him at all, but then the second time, when a group of us went to the margarita bar, I found myself liking him quite a bit. Jeffery can come off as self-important, cocky, sometimes snide. When I met him, he was going to be a big shot. We were all going to be big shots.

His particular area was going to be property development, and Denver was the right town for that. Me, I was going to be a big shot too, though I didn't know in what.

I envied his surety. I wanted it. I envied Michelle's stability and her money and her way of looking at the world. I envied anybody and everybody for reasons big and small.

Michelle was married to a man named Ned, who waved to me from the entryway, who was a lawyer, who was decades into the development of a large belly, who shaved his beard precisely, who helped defend large companies from various harms. They met in college. She got pregnant. It was hardly a love story, and if she had one regret, she said, it was that she had never really experienced either a full-blown romance or a full-blown career. She had middled, she said. I'm a middler, she said. Middle life, middle age, middle field. I didn't see it. To me, she looked as if she had arrived not at the middle but at the prize. Michelle, at fifty-two, was a very handsome woman, with large soft breasts still high on her chest, long legs, square hips and waist, and arms that she worked on at the gym. Her upper lip had thickened slightly, and showed signs of waxing. Ned had gotten the better part of the deal when he married her.

I myself am now approaching fifty-two. I can see it coming toward me, each year a little bigger than the last.

SOME WOMEN I'VE KNOWN have a talent for making and keeping female friends. These are the ones with the big wedding parties and the baby showers and the forty-year anniversary parties, the ones who don't die alone. The husbands in these friendships become something like appendages, or maybe like organs that are hidden, silent, but still deeply necessary. Don't ask me how my kidneys work. I wouldn't be able to tell you. They are just there, as my husband is there, as Michelle's husband was there, doing their work in the background while in the foreground there is the hustle and business of life, of kids, of work, of transportation, of getting dinner on the table, of phones ringing, and bills, and the hard work of the soul. Michelle and I talked about everything, not just about men. We talked about her work—she was a structural engineer, trained at one of the big firms but, at the time I met her, taking just a few clients on the side so as to be available for her recently un-nested family. We talked about mine. We talked about liability and bankruptcy and divorce and diseases and politics and beer butt chicken, which we tried one night to great success. We talked about TV, about how to cantilever a porch, about making scale models, about color combinations, about dreams, about fathers and mothers and siblings, and about a story she read years and years before about a time when the moon was closer to the earth than it is today, so close men in boats would row out to it and one would hold the ladder while the other would climb to the top, then fling themselves forward and turn and land perfectly on the surface, where they would collect moon cheese, which they flung back down to earth with spoons.

I've since found this story, and read it—I didn't know it was as famous as it is. During the reading—only a couple months ago, actually—I had that odd sense of time folding in on itself, because as I was reading I had the feeling of having read it before, at the same time that I remembered Michelle, her voice as she told me about the moon, and the image of the moon in the sky as big as a dinner plate, that image transposed over the picture of my childhood home, the home I grew up in, so that when the story described ducking when leaving the house for fear of bonking your head, I pictured myself ducking into my house as a child, before I knew that the moon is always where it is, and that the earth turns always in the same ways. We talked about everything, but we didn't talk about her husband or her marriage, which was why I didn't tell her that once, while living in Denver, her husband approached me in the kitchen of my apartment while Michelle had run back to their condo for a forgotten bottle of wine. He came up behind me and placed his hands on my hips, lightly. When I turned, his lips were there, and for a moment we kissed. I'm not not accepting responsibility, but had I known his lips were there I would have evaded, wiggled away. His lips were there, and I had the tickle of his trimmed beard on my chin, and for a moment we kissed, and then we separated.

"Why would you do that?" I had asked.

I was more curious than angry.

He might have said, "Why not?" He might have said, "I'd been wondering." He might have said that he thought I wanted him to kiss me, or that life is too short, or that he didn't know when he'd have the chance again. I don't remember what he said. My heart was in my feet.

He went to the bathroom to wash his hands, then ignored me for the rest of the evening, and the week after that, and the month following, so that by the time I went to Arizona I was sure he had forgotten that one moment, forgotten it so completely that he had also forgotten me. I was just one of his wife's friends, one of the women his wife collected. She had had other friends like me. I occasionally heard their names. I could stay, I could go, like a cat.

During my visit to Arizona, he offered to take me out golfing, and at Michelle's urging I went. We talked about his retirement, and about the nuances of corporate mergers, about a friend of his who had dropped dead of a heart attack two months ago, about greens keeping in the desert. We did not talk about the other matter, but I would be lying if I didn't admit to putting on my makeup before golfing, not because I wanted him to kiss me again, but because I wanted to know that if I wanted him to, I could make it happen. It has since occurred to me that if he kissed me in the way he did—so suddenly familiar, his hands on my hips, without passion almost, almost as a matter of right—that he had most likely kissed other women in the same way. Michelle probably knew. They might have even talked about what he did when he wasn't with her. If he had had his affairs—his romances—she never mentioned them. Their marriage, that corner of her heart, was hidden to me.

MICHELLE AND I WENT to the mall. In Arizona, the malls were like space ships, air-conditioned, neon-lit, echoing, as foreign a location as I've ever been in, which is the trick about malls. They make you foreign even to yourself. We got a cup of coffee and shopped first for me, then shopped for her. When I tried on the pants I ended up buying, she said, "Yes. Yes. You." She bought them. It was easy for her and hard for me, and she didn't have her own children around to pamper, she said. "Now you help me." She tried on dress after dress. "Something to make me look pretty," she said. She narrated her aging to me. First you notice it around the eyes. Then on the hands, while driving. Then a certain girth in the stomach that wasn't there before. Not fat, but girth. The legs develop a jiggly layer that won't go away. The skin changes, permanently spotted, thinning, poring up. The hair gets wiry when it goes gray. Dye doesn't help. The breasts fall. The fat in the breasts loses its form. The nipples point down. The skin between the breasts develops small bumps, like moles but not moles, which the dermatologist can remove. The chin grows hairs, first one or two, then three or four, each of which comes in its own time at its own particular location, and must be watched out for, vigilantly. Terrifying. Sometimes, while putting on makeup, you look at yourself in the mirror and catch yourself sideways. You happen to see the skin below your chin, along the tendons of your neck, and you notice how it pulls in a specific way, as if it was both thinner and thicker than it once was. The tendons on your neck, they themselves create wrinkles. All of this happens, while on the inside other processes are taking hold. Dairy doesn't sit as well as it once did. Bread. A night drinking now equals three days of bad sleep. Young people don't look at you—at me—at all any more. A non-entity, you don't exist. There's no roadmap for a woman growing old.

"I'm trying too hard," she said, coming out of the dressing room. "You think I'm trying too hard?" The dress she had chosen was a loose A-line skirt, paired with a tight V-neck top, and a bright red belt in the center.

"I think it looks great."

She turned to look at her back in the mirror, then turned forward again and made herself concave.

"I'm trying to look thirty. You try it on."

I stood behind her and pulled the belt tighter.

"It looks great."

"Come on, try it on."

"It's perfect on you."

Michelle asked the girl helping us to find the same dress in my size. The girl came back with it on her arm.

"Humor me," Michelle urged. "I've got a second wind."

In the dressing room, I stripped down and put the dress on, then walked out on my tiptoes to show her.

She clapped. She had changed, too, and was now wearing another combination of skirt and top.

"It's perfect," she said. "You'll need a different bra."

"It looked better on you," I said, though it didn't. It looked like two different dresses on each of us. I let my feet fall flat.

"You should wear heels," she said.

The girl who was helping us said, "What's your size?"

"I don't need heels. Where would I wear heels to?"

"You're twenty-five. You can wear heels anywhere." She placed her palms on her belly. "I think I'll get this. Do you agree? Doesn't matter. I'm getting it anyway. And the dress for you, and the dress for me."

"You're twins," the girl who was helping us squeaked.

"It's too much."

"Shush."

"I'll just ring you up," the girl said.

On the drive back home, Michelle said, "Good. I feel better. I needed that. I haven't felt this good in years. Never underestimate the power of a new dress. My grandmother used to say that. I finally know what she means." And then, a little while later, with the air conditioning going and the rows and rows of single-story shops passing to our left and right, Michelle said, "There's a man I want you to meet. I thought I'd invite him over to dinner."

FOR YEARS, I REMEMBERED the man's name as Jacob, though recently, going back through some old emails, I discovered it—the name—again, and remembered that it had been Jeff. Jeffery, my husband. Jeff, the man who I met one night at dinner in Arizona, many years ago. It's a common name, so I don't put much stock in the overlap, but I'm surprised that I'd forgotten, or transposed one name for the other one. Jacob is an angel. Jacob is a savior. I don't know who Jeff is, or where the name comes from, or why our paths crossed that night. He had blue eyes with dark black hair that badly needed a cut. To dinner, he wore beige khaki shorts and a button-down blue shirt, decorated with small pineapples. We had seen not that shirt but shirts like it at the mall. He was a builder, which was how he knew Michelle. He had just started his own company, and his wife had either died or was pressing for a divorce, I don't now remember. He drove a truck, a silver truck that we could hear pulling into the driveway. We were both wearing the new dress. "Look at you," Ned had said. "Matchy matchy." He kissed her on the side of her neck, by her shoulder, before he went away to watch TV.

The other man—Jeff—arrived at six with a bottle of wine and his son, freshly washed. The son was maybe nine years old. When the car pulled up, Michelle dried her hands, smoothed her fingers over her eyes, and said, "Well then. Let's see how this goes."

Jeff said some complimentary things about the house, and some things about our dresses, which had immediately started to feel like costuming. Ned made a fuss over the son, and I was introduced, and Michelle offered a glass of apple juice to the boy while Ned opened the bottle of wine. "I don't know much about wine," Jeff said. "I hope it's okay." He was nervous, for no apparent reason. In my brain, I created reasons. A bachelor, unaccustomed to polite company. A widower, still grieving. A suitor, a potential suitor, unsure of his footing. A father, trying to make a good impression with his son. The son came equipped with a video game, which he settled into and kept himself occupied with while dinner finished cooking. "If you're going to play, will you turn off the sound please?" Jeff asked him, and the son turned the sound off right away.

We ate in the living room. The sun was just oranging on the hills to the west, and the ground was still radiating heat. Soon, the air would be just perfect for a cocktail and a slice of cake outside, but not yet. The light from the sunset turned the walls orange then pink then purple, and when the light went entirely from the room Ned got up to turn on the overhead and to open another bottle, our third. I don't remember much of the details of that evening, but at some point we left the living room to eat our cake outside, and Ned made us all dessert drinks, because he took his bartending seriously and he prided himself on mixing the right kinds of drinks.

Eventually, we were all drunk.

Then the moon rose.

It was coming over the edge of the hill in the east, and was as big and fat as I'd ever seen it. Red, too. Red like the sun is red, setting. Red like porcelain is red. A large, red, hot moon, coming over the horizon, the biggest most beautiful moon the universe had ever made, minted new for that night.

Michelle said that when she was a child, she used to think that the moon was closer to the earth than it is now. In her grandparents' age, the moon was close enough to touch, and that the moon pulled the tides so high that the ocean went dry on one side of the world, while on the other side the water was pulled up almost taut, like a bubble.

Ned said, "When I was a boy, I walked to school both directions in the snow."

Jeff said, "The moon is moving away from the earth at approximately the same rate as your fingernails grow. One nano-something a minute."

"Exactly," Michelle said.

"Another drink?" Ned asked the table.

"You're completely lacking in imagination," Michelle said.

The moon had risen above the hills, showing itself in its perfect roundness. For a moment, we all considered it in silence.

"You're probably right," Ned said. "I'm completely lacking."

Michelle said, "Excuse me."

"Arizona," Ned said, pushing back his chair. "It's like this every fucking night."

Jeff and I, alone at the table outside, watched them both go.

"It *is* huge," he said.

Inside, his boy on the couch was punching the buttons on his game, his face lit from below by the screen.

"We're all drunk," I said. "Do you like my dress?" He said he did, and he was probably lying. We went for a walk, picking our way along where no path existed by the light of the moon, and though nothing happened that night between us—no kissing, no touching, nothing actually attempted or performed or asked or answered—there was the feeling that something—anything—was possible, and that if I had wanted him to kiss me, all I would have needed to do was shift my weight and lean sideways, and the kiss would have been as easy as falling, as easy as catching one another on the way down.

But we were all drunk, and maybe my memory is making the night softer and more important than it was. By the time we returned from our short walk the drunkenness seemed to have worn away. Michelle and Ned were loading the dishwasher.

"We went and touched it," Jeff said. "The moon."

"Told you," Michelle replied.

The boy was asleep on the couch by then.

"I should go," Jeff said. He picked up his boy and whispered his goodbyes, then walked down to his truck and put the boy inside. How were we to know? The truck's headlights drew a track on the landscape, before they winked away.

AFTER THE DISHES WERE finished, Michelle made us our beds outside by dragging out the futons and unfolding the light sheets as our tops and our bottoms. She offered to make one for Ned, too, but he declined, so we brushed our teeth and met each other back at our beds by the pool, and one by one Ned turned off the interior lights until there was just his bedroom above us, which eventually went dark too.

Michelle lit a cigarette.

Sometimes, the moon's horns came so near the earth you felt you could hang your laundry on them, and that reaching up you could grasp them like a bar and lift your feet off the ground.

She told me that night about her great romance, the one she had started a few months before I arrived in Arizona. She used all the words a woman uses when she's describing love. She didn't tell me who her lover was, or how she had met him. No details. But she said that for the first time she felt as if she were really living, and she said that the dress we bought that day was for him, for when she saw him again.

Was it Jeff, I asked. She denied it completely. Now, though, I both believe that it was Jeff, and I believe that it never could have been. Because as Michelle was telling me about her great romance, about the patter in her sternum below her heart where her new love existed, about the re-invention of sex that her new love had given her, about the re-birth and re-kindling and re-invigoration of life that she now was feeling, and as we were going to sleep beneath the moon, the truck that Jeff was driving with his son in the seat beside him, his son's head on his lap, the video game held loosely in the son's sleeping hand, that truck went over an embankment and rolled five or eight times until it came to rest with its wheels dug into the sand. As Michelle was telling me about her plans to wear her dress to meet her new lover, the ambulance was taking Jeff and his son to the hospital, where first Jeff died, and then his son. Then the moon rose to its midpoint in the sky, half the size it had been. All this before we had started to sleep.

I want to feel more about this tragedy than I do, but he was just a man I had dinner with on the night he died, a man I might have kissed had I leaned slightly against him, a man my friend might or might not have been in love with that evening. I wonder, sometimes, how many of the men I've kissed in my life are now dead. I wonder about my husband, which one of us will die first, which one I want to die first. I wonder about Michelle, where she is now, dead or alive, she'd be almost eighty years old, and I wonder why she stopped returning my messages, what I did or didn't do, or whether there is simply a time for all things, and our time was through.

After I left Arizona, I got an email from her with the news about Jeff, and then a few weeks later another email telling me she was going on a long trip, and she didn't know when she'd be back. She missed my wedding, when it eventually occurred. We saw each other once in New York for lunch ten or twelve years ago now, on another hot day in the summer. About her lover she said simply that it all turned into a big mess. Worth it, though, she said. I'm almost as old now as she was when I met her. I gave the dress to the Goodwill years and years ago. Now, I wear two-inch heels, kitten heels they call them, when I want to get dressed up. My husband Jeffery still compliments me on my looks, but he seems not to notice, or care, about the particulars. Sex changes, I remember Michelle telling me, and I'd like to talk to her about how it changes, to ask her questions I didn't know to ask. She told me that the women who hang onto the moon, they stretch out their backs from the long days in the kitchen, and the men compete over who can do the most pull-ups, and one by one they fall off until the last ones hooked tight let loose their grips and must be fished dripping out of the sea.

No Choice at All

Sage Cohen

TOMMY HOLDS HIS GUITAR high, over his heart, and moves through my life in 4/4 time. I don't know how tall he is, but if I tilt my head back I can kiss his neck right up under his chin. We meet during the days, because I work from home and he works at night. If I am not available he makes me available. Gets under my desk and between my legs while I am on a conference call. I click the mute button. My throat is the neck of his guitar—pouring music where he presses. He strums his tongue right through me.

To make it clear he isn't my boyfriend, Tommy declares that I shouldn't expect him to change my car tires. But I know he'll do anything I ask. I never ask.

Tommy knows how to please an audience almost as well as he knows how to please a woman. He has a charm and humor that most people confuse for kindness. It is never safe to assume an artist is anything like his art. Who is Tommy when he isn't on stage? When he isn't in my bed? I have no idea.

I MET TOMMY WHEN I went to collect my coat from Matt's place. The truth is, I invented the coat because I wanted a reason to see Matt again. But he was out. A bleach-blond guy in a peeled-down wetsuit—the bass player from Matt's band—let me in. The make-believe coat was nowhere to be found, and I ended up sitting cross-legged on the floor in a see-through dress in a circle of rumpled guys passing around a bong: the rest of the band.

I had stumbled upon these guys the night before when I wandered into the Full Moon Saloon with my notebook, in my pajamas, intending to free write while my just-dismissed boyfriend was at home throwing his belongings into his truck. Tommy, who could easily be confused for a Harley-Davidson gang leader, was the rhythm guitar player. His voice a shock of terra cotta. Matt played lead guitar. When he saw that I found my notebook more interesting than his band, he set out to compete with the free writing. And he won.

Tired of waiting for Matt to materialize in this haze of astonished men, I stood up and Tommy walked me out. As I released the front door he took my hand, pulled me into his chest, and kissed me. Hard. I took that kiss all the way in. I ran to my car without looking back.

As THE MONTHS PASS, Tommy starts to feel real. My pets recognize him. We order in sushi. We walk my dog through the dusty eucalyptus trails of Golden Gate Park holding hands. We argue over vegetables and meats and television and sports. He insists my poetry should be my first priority. But I have cats and bills and I don't believe life is something you give up for art. Tommy can't understand. He's never wanted anything but music and its currency of women.

We drive down the coast to Pescadero and eat his favorite soup, which is really a blend of two soups—chili verde and cream of artichoke. I make note of his preference for reducing two, unrelated tastes to one.

He starts parking his car in front of my house. Kissing me

in front of people he knows. In front of people he doesn't know. He puts a semi-disguised song about me on his album. I feel like some sort of prize he is flaunting. Am I what Tommy wants, or just an escape route from his other life? I don't think he knows. I need him to know.

I stop answering the phone and the door. Count the days in permanent-marker hatch-marks on my arm. As if the only purpose a day might have is to allow or prevent Tommy from entering. I flop down beside Jami on my living room futon where she has been sleeping for a few months.

"Six days sober," I say too loud, as if I actually believe this could protect me in some way from day seven.

BY THE TIME TOMMY is coming and going from my house daily, I want him to spend the night. I want to call him when I feel like it. I want him to myself. He wants this, too, he says. And to be married to me, with two children: Shane and Cheyenne. We pick a city. We color ourselves in.

But Tommy is already engaged to Rachel. He talks about being engaged as if it is something that happened to him, like getting hit by a truck. They were having a fight, he says, and he thought it would ease the tension. He isn't planning to actually get married, but feels that this is a way of giving Rachel the idea of what she wants.

If you have ever looked at a downtown building in late afternoon and noticed how structure exists where shadow carves away light, then you may understand how loving a man can actually depend on him hurting a woman he loves. You want to save her, you want to beg her forgiveness, you want to destroy her. The only pain you can feel is your own.

WE WALK THE FOUR blocks from the beach toward my house, my dog's wet belly spattered with sand, tongue hanging out around his tennis ball. As we approach the corner of Lawton and 44th, Tommy starts retelling our favorite story.

"Remember how those punk kids got out of their car right there, thinking they would intimidate you?" he asks, gesturing into the intersection. The line of his mouth hardens and the muscles lift in his upper arms as his hands make fists.

"Well, I deserved it. It's hard for me to see the stop signs sometimes," I say into his open mouth.

"I'm counting on that." He traces my eyebrows. It's a thing he does. A reassurance that my face is really in his hands. My eyes on him.

"Then you saved me from those terrible boys," I say in my best helpless princess voice.

"Damn straight, I did. No one's going to fuck with my woman on my watch."

The words *my woman* rise to my surface like a buoy on the ocean. A bright little warning.

We turn the corner onto my street. I have his long, black hair wrapped around my fist at the back of his neck. A habit of mine.

When Tommy makes a guttural sound and starts staggering back toward the beach, he sort of drags me with him. Then he pivots us back to where we started. I don't understand what's happening.

"It's her car," he says.

We stand there for a moment. I let go of his hair. I cease to exist as his body organizes into some kind of agreement and he charges into my house without looking back.

IT COULD BE ARGUED that I levitate across the street and inside where there is no air—only Rachel shrieking. Jami materializes through the curtain of anguish and takes me by the hand. She walks me to my bedroom at the end of a long hallway on the other side of the house. She closes the door and we sit on my bed.

"I let her in," she apologizes. "I didn't know what else to do."

There is a pause in the shrieking in which the tenor of Tommy's voice rises. We can't hear words, only inflection. He is millions of miles away.

"I'm sure she expected to catch you having sex," Jami says as she deposits the tissue box in my lap. "But instead, she had to sit and wait for you to finish walking the dog. Which is even worse, I think. Sex is one thing. Friendship is another."

Jami's diagnosis is punctuated by the sound of Rachel sobbing. I can't seem to catch my breath. Jami covers my ears with her hands in an attempt to mute the fact of my lover's fiancée in my living room. I collapse into her chest. I am an empty riverbank, entirely exposed. We are a tide without water. We rock and heave. Rock and heave. Rachel's small and unworthy chorus.

NEW YEAR'S EVE SEEMS like a gaudy fake when the countdown to a clean slate begins two days later. I haven't heard from Tommy, but I know where he'll be tonight, keeping his promise to the one relationship he holds sacred: his public. Jami tries to talk me out of it, but I can't see that I have a choice. I drive to the Full Moon Saloon alone and take the place I know how to take—in the audience, at the front corner of the bar where Tommy knows to look for me.

He doesn't look for me. I don't dance. I don't drink. I stand in a swarm of throbbing young bodies, waiting for something to happen that makes sense. To be struck down for this villainous thing I have done and seem to be intent on continuing to do. Or to be publicly chosen by Tommy and therefore somehow absolved of my complicity.

When it's time for the kiss that makes the crossing from old year to new, the band guys pull their girlfriends on stage. Tommy drifts into the shadows behind the drums. The crowd is cheering like mad for this charade of monogamous love.

It occurs to me that rescued or destroyed are not my only two options. I drive home.

"What did you expect him to do? Pull you up there and kiss you in front of everybody?" Jamie is so small and slender that lying flat on her back on the futon, she seems to disappear into it.

I lie down next to her, as if we were in a field looking at stars. So that whatever wisdom she is channeling might also sink into me. But I see only the stained, white ceiling dividing us from the sky.

A man does in bed what he does with his money, Jami once read out loud from a novel she was reading. We interpreted it to mean every small choice we make signals our character. I see Tommy taking cash out of his wallet. The simple violence of his hand entering the sheath's fold and taking from it.

"Tommy does with women what he does with his soup," I say to Jami. "That is what I can expect. Two choices distilled to one choice, which makes it no choice at all."

"Yes," Jami says, though she's never been to Pescadero with Tommy. She takes my hand and we lie like that, steeped in artificial light.

The Last Time

Tammy Lynne Stoner

WE'D ALREADY SHOT UP a few times, with Tracey shooting me up more than me doing it myself because we were moving on to some harder to reach places on my body. Tracey yawned, rubbed her already red lined eyes, and said she was tired and spent and ready for bed.

"We're out of coke," she said.

"Tomorrow's Saturday."

"You coming to bed?"

"No."

She didn't say anything, just moved her hand through her black hair to flip everything from the part to one side. She was aggravated and concerned but more than that, she was tired. She always did more than me in a single shot then shot half as many times as I did so her high was up then down. Mine was more like up up up down up up down.

Tracey stood up. She itched at one of the white sweatbands she had on her wrists and winced. A month earlier she'd slashed her wrists when I tried to leave. Slashed them so badly she needed stitches. That's why she was wearing sweatbands, so the stitches could heal without any notice.

"Babe . . ."

"I'm okay," I said.

I turned around and looked off, out our French doors. Behind me, I heard the bedroom door click shut.

The door was one of those cheap, hollow-sounding plywood doors that had faded spots from who-knows-what on it and fingertip marks on the other side from where you had to push to get it to close. I saw the light go off under the door and looked around our place. Except for the Gatorade bottles that had turned yellow from cigarette butts, we kept it pretty clean. We had a decent second-hand couch from her mother—dark blue, and a coffee table covered with books and stacks of my writing that I compulsively edited, and the French doors that opened to a row of bars about waist-high so no one could fall out.

The bars made what is called a "Juliet Balcony"—which is to say, no balcony at all. Just a place where Juliet could stand with the rails pressing against her legs, and call to Romeo. It was strange to have French doors on a second-story apartment that opened only to a set of bars, but without those doors we would have suffocated during the insane Texas summers.

Tracey was a little taller than me, with straight hair that she'd recently dyed black—something I don't think she would have done if she hadn't met me. She had that way of being direct and intense even though she was introverted. It was how she used her eyes—how she'd make direct eye contact with you while keeping her head turned down. Those strange green eyes with slivers of brown.

She'd recently been put on Lithium and Prozac. The doctor told her she had to stop drinking because alcohol affects the strength of the meds. She stopped for a week or so, but then she started again. She had this plan on how to regulate her meds and still drink.

In our tiny, off-white kitchen that night—in addition to more Gatorade and a neat stack of canned cat food that had been on sale—was a bottle of mini-thins. Mini-thins are basically speed disguised as diet pills. You could buy them at the counter of gas stations near the lighters and the beef jerky. I used the mini-thins during the day to temper my crash from the night before.

My high was dulling. I could feel my body becoming metallic somehow, and I knew I'd crash soon. I drank more Gatorade—the red kind, always the red kind when I was high. My heart was getting quieter inside my ears. That wasn't a good sign. Shit.

I rubbed my hands on my thighs and readjusted the sweaty elastic waistband on my cotton boxers—the lightest clothing I owned. It was amazing to me how hot it stayed into the night. There was no letting up.

I stood and opened the French doors, thinking it might be late enough to make the air outside cooler than the air inside. A weak draft blew in, making me realize how stuffy it was in our apartment. All that desperation.

My eyes ached from being awake so long and from focusing on pulling liquid into tiny needles and poking those tiny needles into tricky veins. My hands itched. My thighs were sore. I needed to get high. I gave no real thought to the next day, only to the next ten minutes.

I stood with my legs against the bars outside and breathed in the night air. A couple fireflies chased each other across the grass below, grass that had to be watered before the sun came up and after the sun went down every day. I always knew what time it was by the click and hiss of the sprinkler system—11 p.m. and 5 a.m.

Breathing in the fresh air felt good. I imagined that I could send it to different organs. People believed you could. So I closed my eyes to give it a try, sucked in a cool-ish lungful, and pushed the air inside my lungs over to my liver and my heart. The organs I was damaging the most.

I think, *At least it's not heroin.*

A few of my friends had started shooting heroin. *That* was dangerous. You shoot then you nod off then—sometimes—you die. With speed, you move faster so, if need be, you can get help.

My hands ached. I flexed them and shook them out.

Ignoring the fresh air and the fireflies and my bed with Tracey, I grabbed our burnt spoon, our dulling needle, the plastic tube of mini-thins, a clean spoon, and a white plate. I poured the mini-thins onto the plate on the coffee table and sat down on the couch, ready.

The mini-thins were small, yellow squares with a line down the middle, like some kind of generic medicine. Using the back of the clean spoon I crushed eight of them up on the plate. They had this coating on them that all pills must have—like a plastic film. You can't see it, but it must be what keeps all the powder together.

After I flattened the pills with the spoon, I carefully removed the barely-seen plastic film, scraping as much of the powder on the back of each tiny piece on to the plate. The insides of the yellow pills were white—white powder.

Eight pills were enough to fit into the spoon to cook. My thought was that, in addition to making it into a shootable liquid, cooking the powder might somehow purify it—that maybe some residue that might be unhealthy would float to the top and I could get it with a tiny edge of tissue. But nothing floated to the top. The mixture just bubbled and cooked as the powder blended into the heated water. It looked the same yellow-brown color of bong water.

I yanked off the little bit of cotton from a Q-tip on the table and dropped it into the liquid on the spoon. The cotton bloated in yellowing fiber groups as it sucked up the liquid. The cotton acts as a filter to stop particles from going into the needle and then into your vein. It was a critical part of the ritual.

I laid the needle on the cotton and sucked the yellow-brown shit up. The syringe filled. I laid down the spoon, tapped the vial to release any air bubbles—even though I'd heard that they don't really kill you if you shoot them—and looked for a good spot to hit.

I was working as a graphic designer at the time so I didn't want to hit the veins on the back of my hands. The veins on my feet were good but I had never done that. The veins were too big. It's like killing a bug. You can do it pretty easily as long as they are small. I couldn't do my feet.

I examined different parts of my body. *Fuck.* Tracey'd already hit the back of my knees a few times and my arms were— no pun intended—shot so I had no choice but to go for the feet.

The tops of most people's feet are sensitive—maybe because they spend much of their time protected in shoes, so when I propped my foot up on the table and started feeling around the top for good veins, I could feel how tender they were. My high was falling, my arms were aching, the needle was loaded and ready, but I was resisting. I couldn't do it.

I checked my arms again. I could only shoot the left one since I was right-handed so I looked all up and down for a spot on the pipelines of veins to hit. I wrapped a bandana around my arm and felt around. There—on the inside of my forearm. That felt like I could get it. I could hit that spot.

I squinted and blinked a few times then checked the direction of the needle to make sure I was going to puncture the skin at the right angle. I double-checked for air bubbles then opened and closed my left fist several times, hoping to raise the vein. I could see it, a few inches down from a series of red marks from previous injections.

I pressed the needle against the spot and went in, but I didn't hit blood. I had to wait until I saw blood go back into the syringe before I shot or I'd waste the load.

"Fuck!" The tip burned. Whatever was in the mini-thins burned.

I tried again, a little lower, painfully moving the needle around under my skin, hoping to hit—but nothing.

"Fuck."

The spots where I tried itched and burned. The marks turned bright red and swelled a little.

I put my foot up on the table again. There they were—a traffic of decent veins. I pressed against one and felt it respond like rubber. My chest tightened the way it did when I was excited, even though I was horrified at the prospect of shooting that vein.

"Okay, ready, ready." I calmed myself down.

I leaned forward and put the needle up to the monster vein. The tip was cold on my foot. I knew it would hurt because the needle was really dull by now and if the liquid burned just from the puncture, I imagined it would feel like fire when I pushed the plunger.

With a pop that almost seemed like I could hear it, the needle went in. A thin line of blood backed into the syringe. Success. I held my breath and slowly pushed.

Despite the pain, nothing on my body moved except my hand on that fucking plunger. The liquid burned so badly that it felt like the needle had been coated in battery acid. I could feel it for a few inches up my foot.

The trains started up in my ears—the sound of a high coming. The stronger the train sound, the bigger the high always was. I laid down the needle and listened for the train sound to fill my ears.

The first stage—the hyper-alterness part of the high—was on. The blood in my body raced to my hands and feet and ears and the bits us Scorpios are known for. I stood still and surrendered to it. The electric here-ness of it.

A fly buzzed near me. I didn't shoo it away. I understood its jittery flight. I appreciated its paper-thin wings. It was as much a marvel as we humans are.

I wanted more air, less humid air, so I walked over to the open French doors. I leaned my face against the glass. It was cool. My focus moved—I stepped back to look at the moon.

It was low in the sky and so bright that it lit up several cotton candy stretches of clouds moving past it. The whole scene was framed in the open space of the French doors like a painting. I could feel that beauty in my chest like an expansion, like my cells were opening up. The feeling moved from my chest to my neck and my stomach, the way the cold from the glass had moved through my fingers.

The night air was crisp and clean, despite the leftover heat from the day. I could taste it—could taste the herbs in it, the pollen. I breathed in as deeply as I could and felt my heart palpitate from both the drugs and the deep breaths.

I had focus in the speed. Focus on what was important. The air around me, the moon, my heart. The fly buzzing somewhere near me. I could hear it louder than I knew it probably was.

My skin felt like it had a thin layer of oil on it, so that everything that touched it lit it up somehow. A small breeze moved over my skin. A fish probably feels the same sensation when it's pulled from water. Its skin so sensitive that even in the intensity of the moment, it feels everything—the air, the sun—as it moves over its body. This high was fucking awesome.

Then—as quickly as that moment came on, the trains drifted off, the moon dulled, and my skin dried back again. I needed another boost. A bigger one.

That's it?

I wondered if I should snort some of the mini-thin powder—or maybe just take the pills, but none of that would give me the train sounds. The goal here wasn't to stay up—the goal here was to get as high as I could. To get so high that I needed to run around the parking lot outside and listen to music, and press myself naked against the cold French doors. To get high enough to feel the whole goddamn world at once.

As much as I hated the needle, I had developed a fetish for it. I was in love with the ritual of the process that led to the trains. I could get stronger trains—a bigger high was just right around the corner. Now that I'd hit my foot, I could hit my foot again. It would get easier each time.

I had twenty-five mini-thins left. Enough for three hits or, I reasoned, two big hits.

I went through the process again, this time crunching and liquefying and shooting twelve mini-thins. When I hit in, the burn was much worse. My whole foot hurt from it. I wondered if it might be something that could cause me to lose my foot but then the trains hit and I was high—higher than last time, but not as high as I got with coke. I lay back on the couch and felt the world again in the way you feel it when you're that high.

Before the high even winded down, I was crunching pills. This time I propped my right foot up on the coffee table and shot there, glad the elevation made the vein go down a bit.

It was late by the time the third shot surged through me. This one made me feel sick to my stomach and caused my heart to beat so fast I thought I might have a heart attack. I ran through what I knew were the symptoms of a heart attack: nausea, left arm pain, chest pain. My arm throbbed but it didn't hurt. The nausea hit me again like a shock, then left.

I wondered if I should wake Tracey up or call 9-1-1, or what. I tried to stand up but got too dizzy. My heart—the muscle— hurt in a way that felt hot and electric.

I leaned forward on the couch and focused on my breathing. I thought my breath could lead my heart into a slower pace and then I'd be able to move to the bedroom and lie down. The trouble was that if I didn't breathe fast enough my heart would rebel and double-time.

I don't know how long it took, but I managed to get to bed by crawling on the floor while keeping a precise, slow breathing pattern. I moved one leg then waited until I could slow my heart again then crawled another step until I finally got to bed.

Getting into bed was trickier. If I kept my head down, keeping the blood flowing to my heart, I figured I would be okay. No sudden movement. With my head kept low—so grateful our bed was a mattress on the floor—I crawled in.

I laid all the way on the edge, making sure not to touch Tracey because by now I was in such high anxiety that anything on my skin would cause my heart to start racing again. I was sweating and it was hot, but I put the sheet on—a uniform surface to calm my excitable skin.

My face flushed. My left arm hurt. My heart stopped for a few beats then slammed back on with a kick drumbeat. I couldn't move anything or my heart would speed up.

I decided I was going to die.

I was going to die and my parents were going to use my death in church as an example of the lifestyle of homosexuals. The selfishness of homosexuals. The self-hating of homosexuals who know deep down inside that they are sinful, ugly creatures who have strayed from God's love. The sad, lonely homosexual. Dying was bad, but that was worse—to be that. To be evidence that they were right.

The fly landed on my ear. It tickled horribly but I couldn't move. The noise it made was so much louder on the edge of my ear. It buzzed away then landed on my cheek. I felt its feet. My ribs hurt. All of my muscles—my shoulders, my back, my thighs—ached from the panic I was trying to contain. And that fly, that fucking fly, kept buzzing away then landing again. At first I thought it was my dead great-grandmother coming to watch over me, but soon I realized it was just a fly and I wanted to kill it, but I could barely swallow without triggering the heartbeats.

Tracey got up around 7 a.m. Thankfully she'd never rolled over to touch me during the night.

Keeping as still as I was, I could only see as far as my eyes could move without moving my head. I watched her—her shorts and the white edge of her stretched out T-shirt and her sweatbands—as she tiptoed around our room, not wanting to wake me. She didn't know I wasn't sleeping, that I was still wavering between living and dying. I couldn't tell her because I was afraid that any movement to talk might increase my heart rate.

I'd held my body perfectly still all night. Now it was morning and I was still fucked. I was wrong, I guess, about the difference between shooting heroin and shooting speed, or in this case mini-thins.

Tracey walked into our living room and with all my strength, I called out her name. One word. She rushed in and then she saw me, *really* saw me.

"Oh my God, oh my—*fuck!*—what's happening?" Her hands pulled at the bottom of her Pixies T-shirt. Her hands were so strong. They were the hands of a massage therapist. The hands of someone who would work on clients during the day and still come home to give me a massage.

I couldn't move my head because I didn't want to use any strength that would require an increase in blood and that meant more heart beats, so I just stared straight ahead. The fly buzzed.

"This won't go on insurance, right?" I whispered slowly. My voice was so low and soft that she had to lean over me to hear.

"What?" Her green eyes were wide and scanning the room, as if there was something in there to save me. She was breathing in short breaths.

I said, "I'm going to have a heart attack."

She looked behind her, through the open door and into the living room and the detritus of last night. "What did you do— what were you shooting last night? Is that—are those, did you shoot *mini-thins*?"

Her eyes were a panic. She ran her hand through the side of her messy morning hair. I looked ahead and saw the red patches from razor burn on her thigh—such a bitch to shave in this heat. The faint blue pen heart that I had drawn on her leg a few days ago, when we were at a club and she had had to wear shorts because of the heat. She hated shorts. She loved layers and layers of clothes, but this heat. So I drew a heart on her leg and told her how much I liked her leg, that I hadn't seen it in a while.

"Tell them that's all I shot. Not cocaine. That's illegal. Call them. Say that. Only that."

"Oh my God, are you really dying? Shit—I'm calling 9-1-1. Oh, babe . . ." She ran her hand through her hair again. She was okay when anything happened to her, but she freaked out when anything happened to me.

My heart pounded in my ears. I closed my eyes until the spinning caused me to open them again. The fly buzzed around me. I prayed I wouldn't die before the ambulance got there.

I could hear Tracey cleaning up the living room. I heard a match light, no doubt for a candle, and Gatorade bottles being plunked into a garbage bag. I heard her open the front door then run down the stairs to the trashcan.

"Are you okay?" she asked, standing in the bedroom doorway.

"No."

Tracey slowly stepped over to me. She moved to touch my forehead.

"No touch," I managed. I didn't want any stimulation *at all*.

"Okay, okay. I'll sit out here and wait."

A few minutes later the paramedics arrived.

"My girlfriend's in our bedroom. She was shooting up these mini-thins."

"Okay," one of the men said, like this was something that happened every day—and maybe it did.

I was embarrassed when she said she was my girlfriend, ashamed at the way I was portraying gay people. I tried to be cavalier though when they walked into the bedroom.

"Nice to see you," I mumbled from the mattress on the floor.

The shorter, blond paramedic squatted down to talk to me. His knees cracked. "Hi again. Do you remember us? We were here last month, when your girlfriend tried to kill herself. We'll take good care of you."

Instead of acknowledging the paramedic, I focused on the fly buzzing around me. It was all too much—all too humiliating and stupid.

This was my life: I was familiar to the paramedic who was saving me from an overdose because he had saved my girlfriend from a suicide attempt.

The fly buzzed near my head. I lay there. The blond paramedic shooed it away for me. I smelled like metal and sweat. My breath must have been awful.

Tracey told them again what had happened—mini-thins *only*—as they lifted me on to a stretcher and carried me to the ambulance. Our neighbors were watching. The ponytail girl who always wore yoga pants and her ridiculously tall boyfriend, a sunburned redneck guy who spit his chewing tobacco out all over the sidewalk leading to our apartments. The same neighbors who saw the ambulance the month before going into the fucked-up lesbians' place upstairs.

The ride down the stairs on the stretcher was horribly bumpy even though they were carrying it. I focused on the oxygen mask they'd put on me. As long as I had the mask on, I thought, I wouldn't die. After a few jolts on the stretcher, I reached up—the first time I moved my arm on my own in hours—to hold the mask. That familiar panic was creeping into me with each bump. I started praying again.

I didn't know if anyone was listening to my prayers, but I prayed anyway. I thanked Mary and Jesus and God for letting me live, even before they had. I blinked three times hard at Tracey to let her know I loved her. She roughly wiped her tears away and nodded.

The paramedics loaded me into the ambulance with a big bump when the wheels smacked back down from the frame of the stretcher. We were off.

It's No Good Telling Me That

Steve Denniston

I WAS UP AT Shaw's place with Dad and they were talking about a price for taking out the stumps. Dad took his baseball cap off to negotiate. He should have left it on and kept his bald spot covered. It looked bad, starting on top and going to his left. Leave it to my dad to mess up going bald. I wandered back to the truck to wait.

Shaw had all his hair and was dressed nice, ready for the day. It was my dad's button up plaid shirt versus a suit and tie. I didn't wonder who would get the better deal. Shaw wanted a second garage, bigger than the first. Someone had cut down and hauled off all the trees that were in the way. Fifteen stumps remained, all of them the size of a medium Domino's pizza. A week ago, when they were trees, they'd been scrub oak and a couple pines. Too much sun and not enough rain was rough on trees here. There wasn't much pretty about them, full grown or as stumps.

Shaw left in his Audi and Dad came over to me in the truck. He pulled a shovel out of the back." John, you'd better start digging that one there. We'll need to hack at the roots a bit before it comes out."

"You're kidding me right?" I said. "You think I'm gonna pop out that son of a bitch with a shovel? I'd like to know the plan here."

"There was something else I was going to say to Shaw when I was talking to him." Dad leaned the shovel against the truck. "But I don't know what it was."

"This job will take more than hand tools." I jumped in the back of the pickup and threw out an ax, a pick ax, and another shovel. "He wants it done in a week, right?"

Dad walked to the closest stump. "I should have written my thought down. I need one of those little notebooks you can put in your pocket and write things down in. Then I wouldn't forget."

"You were going to write it down while you were talking to him so you could remember to talk to him about it?" I put my hands on top of the tailgate and jumped out of the pickup bed. "There are guys that dynamite stumps. That's their job, you know."

Dad opened the tailgate and sat down. His gut made the buttons on his shirt look like they'd pop off with one more burger. "I'll go back home. We got some chain in the garage. Wrap it around the stumps and then we can pull them out with the truck."

"Get me some black powder, a foot of metal pipe, and five minutes on the internet. We could make our own dynamite."

"Start digging out that first stump. I'll unload the truck for you." He turned around and saw I'd already got the tools out. "When did you do that?"

"Hurry up and bring the chainsaw for cutting through the roots." I tapped the stump with a shovel. "This is going to take forever and I'm not doing the work all by myself."

He got in the truck and left, a forty-five minute round trip to our place and back.

Shaw's house was on a hill surrounded by cherry orchards. The trees had been picked clean at the start of summer. Their work was done. I pulled a hose over from the house to soak the dirt around the first stump. The ground was rock hard. The hose didn't reach far enough so I scraped out a shallow trench, about twenty feet long, leading to the first stump.

It was quiet. That 'outside the city' kind of quiet that always surprised me. No other people, no other cars, none of that background neighborhood noise. Only the birds chirping and squirrels chattering. I was on summer vacation and technically, this was Dad's vacation too. He drove one of the diesel Cats out at the dump shoving huge piles of people's crap around. It was the first job he'd worked at in quite a while where he stayed long enough to earn vacation days.

At the end of the school year he told me he'd take some time off this summer and we could do something together. I thought he meant a road trip. Maybe camping on the mountain.

I kept digging around the stump, making holes for the water, hoping the ground would soften. It made a sludge-filled moat. The dirt was more like clay once it got wet.

Dad barely kept his shit together. I think that's what attracted my parents to each other in the first place. My mom couldn't keep her shit together at all. I haven't seen her in years. She went to New Mexico and we get a message from her on the answering machine every four months or so. My friends think they got a divorce. People understand divorce. No one understands, 'Mom left on Tuesday and doesn't know why. ' She told me that, "I don't know why I had to leave, I just had to leave." She didn't actually tell me that, just left me a message.

There was a root close to the surface and about three inches round. It took some work to dig around each side of it to get a good clean shot with the ax. I got situated with one foot on the stump and the other stuck in the mud so it wouldn't slide. It was an awkward angle, plus trying to strike something right at my feet made it difficult too.

The ax was double sided and not very sharp. The root would be hard, live wood. I took careful aim, raised the ax high, brought it down hard, and missed. Mud splattered all over me, even in my stupid wide open mouth. The temperature was in the high eighties so I left my clothes on, hosed myself off, and lay down to dry in the sun.

An hour later I woke up and started on the same stump again. Dad got back two hours later with some sandwiches. PB & J for me and bologna for him, two sandwiches each. We sat on stumps and ate. He nodded at the one I'd been working on. "How's it looking?"

"Slow. I got four of the big roots cut on the far side." I took a bite of sandwich. Too much peanut butter and not enough jelly. "It should go quicker with the chainsaw."

"Yeah, I forgot the chainsaw. That's something else I could have written down so I didn't forget." He looked up at the sky. It was clear except for lines from jets that went past way above us. "I could go back and get it. I remembered the chain."

"At least you remembered lunch."

"I put some apples on the counter but I don't think they made it to the truck." He looked up at the sky again. If Dad left to go back for the chainsaw I might not see him until dinner. We could make do with the tools we had. I went over to the hose and got a drink. It had that chalky taste of well water.

Dad took a deep breath. "Smell that?"

I shook my head, "No."

"Clean, fresh air. This time of day the garbage pile starts to heat up and you can really smell it. I should find a job that smells like it does out here."

"That job is just fine for you," I said.

We hacked away at every root we could find, then we'd dig a little deeper to see if there were any more roots. "What if we get a stump grinder?" I said. "Don't they have those at the rental place?"

"That would eat our profit," Dad said. "As long as we pull two stumps a day we'll be fine."

"What about some kind of bulldozer? Even a small one. We could pop these out like corks."

"Too bad I can't borrow one from work. Get a D9 in here and we'd be done in ten minutes." Dad leaned on his shovel. "I'm tired of this. Let's get the chain around this one and see what happens."

The chain was left by whoever rented our house before us. It looked like it was for securing loads on log trucks, thick and rusted with big hooks at each end and too long for what we needed. Dad wrapped it around the stump three times and we still had a good twenty-five feet of it. I secured the other end to the trailer hitch.

He got in the truck. "Stand behind the stump and tell me if it's moving."

"You forgot to lock the hubs." I went to the front wheels and did it for him. "Put it in low too."

I walked to the other side of the stump. Dad pulled forward until there wasn't any slack in the chain, dropped the truck into low, and gave it some gas. The truck was a diesel, which made it loud when it idled, so when Dad started pulling it got really loud.

The chain tightened and lifted my end of the stump about three inches. Dad gave it a little more gas. The back right wheel slipped, shooting rocks and dirt at me, but the stump didn't move any more. He let the truck roll back a few feet and stuck his head out the window to look at me. The whole area around me stank from diesel fumes.

I held my hands apart to show him how far it moved. "Want to try it again?" I said.

He grinned. "It ain't revved until the rods are thrown." He pointed to the back. "Get in and stand over the wheel that slipped. Bounce on it when I give it some gas so we can get some traction."

I climbed into the pickup bed. Dad pulled forward again, I bounced in the back corner over the tire, and the stump lifted up again, a bit farther this time. I shouted, "Keep going!"

Dad goosed the gas in time with my jumps. The stump lifted more, a root snapped, and the whole thing popped out of the hole. The truck jumped forward. My knees slammed into the tailgate. Dad hit the brakes and I fell backward into the truck bed. He turned around to look and I gave him a thumbs up, "We did it."

He let out a 'good old boy' whoop, took the truck out of low, floored it, and cranked the wheel. He kept honking the horn. I sat up and pounded the side of the truck screaming, "We did it." We spun a tight donut in the dirt with the stump bouncing behind us getting tangled in the chain. The truck hit a slick patch from the water. The tires slipped and Dad let off the gas. We lurched to a stop.

The stump kept swinging along the arc of our turn. Brown wood spinning, mud and dirt flying, the rusty chain still attached to the back of the truck. It whipped around tight and fast, and slammed into the front wheel on the passenger side. The truck shivered sideways.

Dad turned off the engine, rolled up his window, and stared straight ahead. We were facing Shaw's house. It was bright green with white trim. Almost the same green as his over-watered lawn.

The stump was about a foot off the ground, halfway into the wheel well. The tire was turned in at an angle it was never meant to go.

I jumped out of the back and went over to Dad's side and knocked on the window for him to get out. He nodded his head yes and got out of the truck. Two apples rolled off the seat and fell to the ground. I put my hand on the bottom edge of the truck and got down to pick them up. Dad slammed his door shut, right on my fingers.

"Oh for fuck's sake," I shouted.

"What? Oh darn it all." He yanked on the door. "It's locked."

I pounded on the truck with my other hand. "Unlock it."

"The keys are inside."

The pain in my fingers pulsed. Dad stepped back and punched the window. His fist bounced off. I put my face against the side of the truck. "Do something." He ran away. The bit of my fingers sticking out of the truck were bright red.

He came back with the ax, smashed in the window, and unlocked the door. I pulled my hand out. It was like my fingers weren't fingers anymore, only pain.

I sat down, kind of falling into a sitting position. My hand hurt even more when I jarred against the ground. All four fingers had a deep red crease from the door. Dad bent over and held his hand out. "Let me see." I put my fingers on his palm. His hands were still bigger than mine.

He bent down further to get a closer look. "Uh oh." His face was white and his forehead was covered in sweat. "I shouldn't have looked."

He kept bending down, tried to steady himself against the truck, and passed out.

I moved my hand out of the way and let him hit the ground.

I'd seen him pass out before when visiting people at the hospital. They weren't even that sick. He hated those police forensic shows, wouldn't watch slasher movies, and sometimes real life was too much for him.

I walked over to the hose and sprayed him until he sat up. His face was still pale. He pointed at my hand. "I think you're going to lose a nail or two."

"My fingers might be busted, you know."

"Broken bones I can take. But a fingernail falling off? Even the thought makes me queasy." He stood up. "I need some ice for my hand. Something happened when I punched the window."

"Your hand?" My fingers were already swollen. I went up

to the house, turned the water off, and circled around Shaw's place. The whole front of the house was made of five-foot tall windows that were low to the ground. One was open and its screen popped off easy. I tossed my muddy shoes into the yard and climbed into the living room.

The windows looked out on the Columbia River Gorge, over the thirteen thousand people in The Dalles, and off toward the dam holding back all that water. A big sectional couch and three oversized chairs were turned toward a wall where a huge TV was mounted.

The doorbell rang. I let Dad in and told him to take off his boots. In the kitchen I got two mixing bowls, filled them with ice water, and took one to the living room. I turned a chair to face the windows, sat down, and stuck my hand in the ice. It made it hurt worse.

Dad came in with his bowl of ice water. He was wearing his T-shirt and underwear. I shook my head. "What?" he said. "My clothes are wet." He sat down on the floor next to me and stuck his hand in his bowl. "Can you believe that stump? Probably have to replace the whole wheel, tie rod, and the axle. Think we'll have to replace the axle?"

There were white caps down on the river. It was blowing pretty good if we could see them this far away. Up here it was calm, like the wind was blowing right around Shaw's property so it wouldn't get disturbed.

"Sorry about your fingers," Dad said. "I'm a terrible parent, huh?"

My smashed fingers were slightly curved. I willed them to straighten. They didn't even quiver. I was going to live the rest of my life with a deformed hand to remind my father of his idiocy. At least there was some comfort in that.

I said, "We need to find a phone and call someone to get us to the ER." It's not that I'm the only kid in high school who doesn't have a cell phone. It's that Dad is the only adult in the whole town who doesn't have a cell phone.

He scratched his shoulder. "Everyone I know is working."

"Call work then. See if someone can get us when they're done."

"No hurry. It'll be an hour before anyone heads in from the dump." He held up the hand he'd been icing. "Check out my knuckles. They're bruising pretty good." Two knuckles were slightly blue, probably from the ice water.

"When your mom left us the first time," Dad said, "I punched a hole in the wall each month she was gone. Every night on the 14th I'd find a good spot in between some studs and slam my fist right through the sheetrock."

"Maybe someone at your work came in early. You could always try and call." I lifted my hand out of the water to let it warm for a minute.

"I'd patch up the hole that night. Kept a sheet of drywall in the laundry room." He popped an ice cube in his mouth and crunched it up. "Did it real slow and careful. I got so good I didn't even have to sand it down the next morning. Used a sponge to feather the mud out."

He had never told me about punching and patching holes before. Whenever we looked at a house or apartment to move into, Dad always rated it by how good the drywall looked. Once he told me, "You can see every seam on the walls and ceiling." He had turned around and walked out. "We're not living in a place that can't do drywall right."

Dad pointed at a hummingbird that flew right up to the huge windows in front of us. "Your mom came back seven months later. The day after you turned four. She was mad that I didn't wait one more day for you to open presents. I didn't even know she was coming back."

"Maybe Terry could come get us," I said. "Doesn't he always try and sneak out early?" My fingers throbbed in time to my heartbeat.

"Do you remember that birthday? It was kind of two birth-days. She went out and bought a bunch of Legos you were too young for. We had to go to the doctor because you shoved a red piece up your nose."

"Or leave a message for Mike," I said. "He owes you a favor after we hauled that cord of wood for him."

"I bet you remember that doctor visit. He really had to dig that piece out. You cried like a baby. I didn't pass out, but I threw up in the sink. You remember that?"

"Second grade is the first time I remember her leaving." I swirled my hand in the ice water. "It was spring. She missed my choir concert."

"I tried to be a drunk when she left that time. I wasn't any good at it. I don't know how those guys do it, drinking that much every night. It's so expensive too. I gave up after two months."

"You never drink."

"I don't like the taste of it. Never did."

The skin on my fingers was puckering from being in the water so long. Big fat swollen fingers and wrinkled fingertips. All my friends' dads drank, but not mine. I had always chalked it up to one more weird thing about him.

"She wasn't gone as long that time," Dad said. "Came back next fall in time to take you trick-or-treating."

I had told everyone her costume was a crazy hippy from the Sixties. Except she'd been wearing clothes like that since she'd showed up. And she wore more clothes like that the day after Halloween, and the day after that, and on and on until she left again.

Dad sat criss-cross staring out the window. I had a perfect view of his bald spot and a brown mole on top of his head. If a doctor saw that mole, he'd get my dad all worried that it might be cancerous. I never worry about that. If Dad ever gets can-cer it will be testicular. There's no other way a cancer scenario would play out with him. People would be asking me how he was doing, how far it progressed, how he was handling the treatment. I'd spend all my time talking to everyone I knew about my dad's balls.

"When's the last time you had a physical?" I asked.

He held up his hand and wiggled his fingers. "I'll be fine. You're the one who needs a doctor." He set his bowl on the floor and stood up. "I'll find a phone and see who can come get us. What's my work number?" I would have given him shit for not knowing his own work number, but he'd only point out he never calls work. I told him the number and he walked away repeating it.

The ice in my bowl was half melted. I went back to the kitchen for more. There was an empty base station for a phone on the counter. I pushed the 'Find Handset' button and followed a beeping sound back to the living room. The phone was under a *Time* magazine on the coffee table.

Dad shouted from upstairs, "What's that? An alarm?"

"I found a phone," I said.

"I found some painkillers in the bathroom."

"What kind?"

"OxyContin."

"How about that and some ibuprofen?"

I called Dad's work and the secretary, Roberta, answered the phone. She always made sure Dad got my messages. I asked her if Terry or Mike were there today. Terry had left already and she didn't know where Mike was.

"What's going on?" she said. "Aren't you on vacation with your dad?"

I told her our truck broke down and we needed a lift. She kept asking questions. Where were we? Why were we at Shaw's place? Was anyone hurt? I'd only met Roberta once, at the grocery store. Mostly we talked on the phone and she was nice, but she was a stranger.

She asked again, "Was anyone hurt?"

"Not when the stump hit the truck." I touched my thumb to my middle finger and pain lightninged up my whole hand.

"John, what's going on? Where's your dad?"

"It's not that bad. I got my fingers shut in the truck door, that's all. I'll probably go to the doctor tomorrow if the swelling doesn't go down. It's not that bad."

"I'll leave right now," she said. "It would take forever to find Mike."

"You don't need to come," I said. "We can wait."

"You gave me the address so it's no good telling me that. I'll be there as soon as I can."

She didn't let me say anything else and hung up. I turned around and Dad was sitting on the stairs. His underpants had a rosy tint. He'd probably thrown my red T-shirt in with the whites last time he did laundry.

"That was Roberta," I said. "She's on her way."

"Not Mike? Mike knows lots about broke trucks. His neighbor's a mechanic." Dad held the pills out for me. "Roberta doesn't know anything about trucks."

"No. Probably not." I took the pills and swallowed them dry. "I'm going outside to check on the truck." I was almost through the door when Dad said, "Okay. I'll clean up in here."

When Mom left last time, Dad didn't know where she had gone. "She'll call," he'd said to me. "Once she finds a place."

"She has a place," I said. He didn't answer.

Dad gave up sleep for a while after that. I'd get up in the middle of the night and he'd be in the living room reading a Louis L'Amour novel. A used bookstore sold them for fifty cents each and Dad bought every one. I sorted them by title once and he had quite a few duplicates. I don't think he knew.

He couldn't hold a job for long back then. The sleep he did get happened mostly during the day. You can only call in sick so many times before your boss gets tired of it. One time I came home and he was asleep on the couch again and a message was on the answering machine saying he needed to get his butt into work. I woke him up. "What are you doing? Go take a shower."

"I had a dream," he said, "that you and I were fighting."

"We are fighting," I said. "What would Mom do if she came back and found you like this?"

He sat up. "All we do is worry about when she's coming back. And the moment she comes back that fear flips over and we worry about when she'll leave again."

"This isn't about Mom," I shouted. Then I shouted some other shit and some more shit after that. I was a real jerk to him. He had never told me about punching holes in the wall, or trying to be a drunk.

Dad's clothes were still wet so I moved them into the sun on the middle of Shaw's lawn and put my shoes on. Down by the truck I sat down in the dirt. It was difficult with only one good hand, trying to protect a busted hand. I dropped to my knees and half-fell, half-rolled over. It got me on the ground and I slid under the truck.

The stump still had a lot of dirt on it. Especially on the bottom where the thickest roots left the trunk. Going off those roots were smaller roots, then even smaller. That's why it had been so hard to pull out. We'd cut the big roots that spread away from the stump, but right underneath where some went straight down, that was where it had been holding on the hardest.

I tugged on the wheel to see if anything would fall apart. The stump wiggled more than the wheel did. I picked up a stick and poked the stump. Some dirt dropped down, right into my eye. "God dammit." I shoved the stick into the stump as hard as I could and a dirt clod fell into my other eye. I rolled onto my stomach and rubbed at both eyes trying to make them water.

Dad kicked my boot. "What's up?"

"Dirt in my eyes."

He grabbed both my feet and pulled me out from under the

truck. My shirt slipped up and the ground scraped my belly. He grabbed me under my armpits and lifted me. I'd never have guessed he could still pick me up like that. I kept my eyes shut.

"Put your hand on my shoulder," he said. "I'll walk you over to the hose." I waved my arm around but couldn't find him. "Down here," he said. He put my hand on his shoulder. He was bent over at the waist, almost a ninety-degree angle.

"What are you doing?" I tried to push him up.

He grunted. "Don't do that. My back went out when I lifted you up." He sucked in air and breathed it back out slow. "Come on, let's get you to the water."

I held on tight to him. "Do you have your pants on? You're not walking around in your underwear are you?"

"I got pants on. But my boots aren't laced. Try not to step on the laces." My eyes were stinging and shut tight. We inched our way carefully to the hose. He put it in my hand and left to turn on the water up at the house.

A plane came over the hill and flew right over us. It sounded small, a single engine prop, probably headed to the airport across the river. It was a faint buzz when the water finally turned on, warm from the hose sitting in the sun.

I made myself open my eyes and rinsed them out. The water ran over my head, I washed my face off, and straightened up. My swollen fingers were tingling, they still hurt but the ibuprofen and OxyContin had kicked in.

Dad was by the house shuffling toward me, leaning over with his hands on his lower back. "I'll be right there," I said. He waved a hand to show he heard, but kept walking. He looked so broken, bent over like that, but he kept coming toward me.

Tessa's Drought

Cindy Williams Gutiérrez

AFTER MAMA DIED, I stopped sleeping. This was after I decided to stop crying. Not for Mama—I couldn't shed a tear for
her—but for all the other bereavements in town. You see, I'm
the town mourner.

It's a small town and I've always taken up too much space.
But this is just one more reason I loved Mama so much. When
someone let loose an unkind word about my size, Mama always gave me a bear hug and bellowed—as if she wanted the
whole town to hear: "Tessa, you're a big-hearted woman. Your
body is the perfect frame for your large heart." Sometimes I'd
try to pull away, to burst free of her arms. She'd hold me a minute longer, then whisper: "It's your smile that worries me—it's
big enough to swallow all the sadness in the world."

That's how I became the wailer at town funerals. If I could
smile away other people's pain, I might as well cry it away, too.
People say when I wail at funerals, my round body rumbles
and shakes—as if the earth itself were mourning.

But not one tear for Mama. It's like a switch had been
flipped. All I could manage was to greet each morning with

stone-dry silence. After I dragged myself out of bed, each day was a blur. And when darkness finally came, sleep evaporated. I could only mourn in the dark, though it didn't sound at all like wailing.

As soon as I closed my eyes, I started concentrating on Mama's particulars. I couldn't help myself. Maybe it was the quiet all day long. But when I tucked myself under the flower quilt Grandma made for Mama, I distinctly heard Mama's organ-pipe voice. Before I knew it, Mama and I were reliving entire conversations. And soon we began to have new ones.

A month after her death, I said, "Mama, I have to tell you something. You're not going to like it." She said to go ahead, she was listening. I gulped, then spat out the words: "Flora's Flowers is closed. I put a CLOSED—INDEFINITELY sign on the door of your shop today." At first, she didn't say much. But I could tell she was smiling. Then she said she knew I knew what was best. I could never contain myself when she listened so close like that, so I kept going: "Mama, I love our talks. But I feel like I'm in the middle of a tornado. A great big tornado that sucks me up every night. I just keep whirling through the air, blind, with no place to land." She said I'd find what was best.

That's when I began to give everything a try. There had to be a way to coax sleep. Warm milk with a drop of vanilla and a dash of cinnamon. Hot oats sprinkled with goat's milk or fresh cream. A warm poultice of Dead Sea salts applied to my head, then to my chest. Long baths with rain water collected in steel buckets. Lavender essence pressed from the garden behind Mama's shop. Dozens of unscented candles lit in the shape of the number 8 on its side. I tried reading the Bible—its centuries' worth of words to make my eyelids heavy. When all else failed, I rolled out of bed and fell into slow forward bends, my head a planet suspended in space. All in the hopes of floating into a weightless world.

During the following two months, I surrendered.

Wakefulness became a way of life. At first, I stayed indoors. I began lining kitchen cabinets with floral prints. Lilies—Mama's favorites. Then I turned my attention to the walls of my small bungalow. One by one, I painted a strip of wainscoting in each room. Star in the bedroom, tiger in the living room, callas in the kitchen, cannas in the bath. I reserved Easters for the laundry room that doubled as my wailing room. This is where I used to practice yawling, accompanied by the dryer's thump… thump. It reminded me of a large heart, beating.

During the second three months of mourning, I remained dry-eyed. But I ventured outdoors. For hours I stared at my hapless garden, which stared back—empty, except for weeds.

Mama had opened her flower shop the day she discovered she was pregnant with me. She said that after *Mama*, my first words had been *mum*, then *spider, sun, flower*. I named my first dolly with the black eyes Susan. But by the time I started school, I had no use for flowers. It wasn't that I hated them. I just didn't care about them. They needed too much care. You had to water them, feed them, handle their petals delicately. And after all that care, they didn't bother to last. So why should I bother? They lost their beauty in the blink of an eye and became unsightly. Even at the height of their beauty, they were messy: their stems and leaves produced a green goo that stuck to the sides of plastic containers and glass vases alike. And their fragrance? Gardenias made me dizzy and lilies—well, lilies made me nauseous. They repulsed me.

By the time I turned thirteen, all flowers seemed like nothing more than silent prima donnas. I especially disliked mums during Homecoming, and later, roses around prom time. And I grew to hate yellow, thin-petaled flowers most of all.

But there was one flower I could stand. The morning glory. When I was a little girl, Mama told me that it slept at night. She said it curled its petals inward like wings so it could nest in the dark. Then, on my sixteenth birthday, Mama gave me the key to the shop, and the key to my secret wish.

"You run ahead, darlin'. Today you can open the shop by yourself. I'll be just a few steps behind you."

For the first time in my life, I ran like the wind. I unlocked the front door and flipped the sign to OPEN. Then I threw open the back door and ran through Mama's garden. I ran straight to the morning glories, hoping to see them open their petals wide to the world. Day after day, all through high school, I tried. I got up earlier and earlier. I skipped breakfast. I ran faster and faster. But I never caught them in the act. And for the better part of two years, I became what I never dreamt possible—thin. Though my newly slim wrists never showed off a corsage.

UNDER THE MOON'S STARING eye, the weeds looked like thousands of spiky fingers pointing at me. I wondered aloud if my fleshy arms could lift the forty-pound bag of mulch, push the wheelbarrow filled with loam, and dig up the clay soil with hoe and shovel. I decided to find out. It wasn't long before I spent my nights amending the soil, sprinkling seeds, and cutting new rows. In three months, I had buried thousands of seeds in an acre of what had once been barren ground.

The last three months were for watering. For the first two, I made a schedule for myself and kept to it during the hours I was clear-eyed: 1 a.m. the front, 3 a.m. the back, and 5 a.m. the quarter acre I called the back forty. I bought more flashlights and kerosene lamps. I discovered hose extenders. And I learned to predict the howling of coyotes on the day before a full moon. Dry-eyed, I watered and watered.

In the final third month, the seeds began to sprout. I kept watering. The stems grew taller, the buds fuller. I continued watering. I scoured my fields for one open bud. Nothing. I watered and watered.

On the day before the last full moon in the ninth month of

mourning, I watered the back forty. There was a strange quiet on this night—no coyotes. Suddenly a shot rang out, followed by a yelp and scramble through brush. To my right, down the ravine toward the creek, I heard a soft whine, then a low moaning. I dropped the hose and for the first time in thirty years, I ran.

As I bushwhacked my way down to the ravine, the moaning grew louder and louder, and the whine less regular. By the time I arrived at the creek, my arms were covered with cuts and my knees ached. There, in front of me, a coyote bitch bared her teeth.

The pup lay on its side, breathing heavily. To get a better look, I took one small step to the left. The bitch growled. I stiffened and avoided eye contact with the mother. She stared at me until the pup's breathing changed. The bitch began to lick her pup and moan quietly. I took up the moan. I felt the chords vibrate in my throat for the first time in nine months. It was as if my insides were trembling with sound. I moaned louder and louder. The coyote moaned louder, too. I began to howl and wail. The coyote howled and wailed louder. And when I thought I had no more tears and no more sound, the two of us bayed until the unblinking moon disappeared.

Just after my first wail—and before the coyote's, the pup had stopped breathing. The coyote lay motionless next to her pup. Even when I came closer, she didn't move. I reached out a hand to stroke her fur. Then I stopped, and left them to their own.

I made my slow way up the ravine. It was steep and rocky, but I took no notice. My body was still vibrating with sound. When I reached the top, the sun was beginning to rise. Streaks of light nearly blinded me. Squinting against the glare, I looked across the field in search of the spot where I had left off watering. I couldn't find it. All I saw was a sea of blue morning glories extending their petals to the sun.

Real World Reject

Trevor Dodge

I WAS THE ONE they didn't pick to live in the loft.

The one not picked to live with seven strangers.

They didn't want to know what happens when I stop being polite.

When I start getting real.

This is the true story.

I am not alone in this, but I was the one they never even considered.

The one married and middle-aged.

The one they were afraid would bring a mortgage into the loft, maybe.

Afraid would move a husband and children in, too, maybe.

They weren't interested to find out what happens when nothing at all happens, when people never stop being polite, when there are bedtimes and routines and the mailman brings mail that has to be opened.

That's what I would do every day.

Open the mail.

Open and sort the mail for everyone in the loft I wasn't

picked to live in.

I wouldn't snoop.

I would help.

Help the others who were picked to keep on top of things, help them organize and prioritize their obligations.

Is that why they didn't pick me?

Or is what happened is I was picked at first and they showed me to the other strangers who'd already been picked and they all decided not to let me be picked for real, for keeps?

All of them felt this way?

Except for the mousy bi-curious one, or the churchy one, or the cowboy hat one, or the lip-pierced one, or the community college one?

Is that what happened?

Or is what happened more complicated?

Is what happened that everyone picked me to be picked, and they all agreed, but then the pickers asked my friends, my family, my priest, my boss, my exes, my currents, and they all told such compelling stories about how the adverse effects for them wouldn't be worth it?

That ultimately the drama would be too much about what happens outside the frame and not what happens inside it?

That the parts they couldn't film or hint at, these parts weren't or wouldn't be parts at all?

Or is what happened that they friended me on Facebook as someone I thought was really that someone, but really they weren't that someone at all?

And they followed me and they read my status updates and they looked at my photos and then didn't read my status updates and then didn't look at my photos anymore?

What if that was it?

Was it something someone else posted about me?

Or didn't?

Was it a private message sent by someone who I have no

contact with anymore, someone who said I wouldn't fuck any-one in the loft?

Or that I would fuck everyone in the loft?

Did any of them want to fuck me?

Were they asked this before they got to pick whether or not I'd be picked?

Was it a tight contest between me and that other person who didn't get picked to be picked either?

The one who, given the right light and drink and room, I could fall desperately in love with for three minutes?

The one who could make me more real, less polite, the one who I'll never meet in any other way, the one who won't ever meet me?

Maybe no one wanted to fight me.

Maybe that's what really happened, what's at the heart of everything.

They aren't afraid of me, because they know they shouldn't be.

They just don't think I'm worth the fight, no matter what it's about.

Not if it's about taking out the garbage or unclogging the toilet or doing the dishes or asking ill-timed questions or mak-ing up rumors or breaking girl code or not breaking girl code or setting the alarm or camping on the computer or moving around the furniture or squeegeeing the shower or piling the laundry or scooping the dog poop or being a tease or being too forward.

Not being forward enough.

Not liking her instead of him.

Not liking him instead of other him.

Not liking him at all.

Not liking any him.

But I do and I don't.

That's why I open the mail, you see.

I open the mail because I have to know more about myself.

There's more in the mail than just what other people want.

And that is why I wrote you today.

A real letter.

On paper.

Crisp folds.

Perfumed envelope.

Stamped.

Licked.

With ink and everything.

And I hope you feel like I meant it when I wrote it, when I wrote all this by hand and smudged the paper with the knuckle of my pinky.

Stained my knuckle so bad my husband and kids and boss all thought I'd punched someone.

Bruised it.

Which of course is always what happens when you're writing faster than you can think.

But that's just me making excuses again.

Because that's what always happens.

Because that's what I do.

Gore Junkies

Jennifer Williams

EVEN WITH THE STORM coming, she can hear kids outside, laughing and shouting like there's plenty of time. Their game seems to move them from door to door, and by the voices she pictures an unruly cluster advancing, pausing to conspire or bicker, sometimes doubling back.

The blinds inside are twisted closed but the window panes are thin; the door doesn't really seal shut. In the small room, the bed is shoved near the window with only a narrow gap to stand. When the voices approach, the wall seems little more than a curtain. He groans and covers his face with an elbow, but she lifts her head.

"Sure." She settles back, against her pillow. "I dream about you."

He says, "Like what?" still covering his eyes. They're naked except for her jewelry: a beaded necklace and a wedding ring. Tattoos mark both his shoulders and she can see one now, the medieval battle ax—a first-film souvenir.

"You won't like it," she says.

He lowers his arm. "Tell me anyway."

"Remember last month? I told you I woke up angry?"

"Said you were shaking from it."

She nods. "My house has this big glass door. I stood there, I don't know how long afterwards, watching all the taillights make tracks."

"You can see traffic?"

"On a few roads. We're up pretty far."

"Must be quite a view."

"My feet got cold," she says. "I remember that."

He toes the bunched sheet at the end of the bed, raising his left foot, dropping it back down. "So, this dream. I made you *angry*?"

"You had a heart attack."

"I'm *thirty-two*!"

"Don't remind me."

He reaches over, brushes her cheek. "You're fine," he says, and she stifles a groan. "But why am *I* dying in your dreams?"

"I didn't say you died."

He sits up partway. "Recovered?" His eyes are hopeful, like this is real. "Hey! Were you my nurse?"

"I'd never have that dream." She pushes him back down, a little too hard, and he catches her eye. "Anyway, some guy threw a can at your head."

He laughs. "Why a can? Was it in a bar? Because then you'd think, bottle."

"This isn't a scene, Mr. Director. It was my dream."

"*Writer*-director, if you don't mind."

"You were on a promo tour," she says. "Playing the indie artist somewhere. Winston-Salem, Dallas, maybe. I remember the room had all these little windows, but they were up too high. Only good for light."

"Like in Toronto?"

"Maybe that's where I got it from. The hall with all those velvet chairs." She rubs her fingers against a thumb.

"That big room? And it was *my* interview? Man, I'm even more famous in your dreams."

"I'm sure it wasn't packed."

"Can't get all the details right," he says. "So, the can?"

"Well, it smacks your forehead, straight out of professional wrestling."

"Or a skit with truckers! Some meathead slamming it, accordion style, on another guy's head." He grins. "Tell me I got that much, at least."

"Nope, yours just bounced off—ping."

He gapes, like this is worse than the heart attack. "Are there any *good* parts to this dream?"

"It was one of your stalkers. The guy who always calls you buddy. At first he was faceless, just a T-shirt and jeans, you know? Then I recognized him. Then it was like I'd always known. Why are dreams like that?"

He wiggles his eyebrows. "The stranger that isn't a stranger."

"Right. But a guy we'd known to look out for." She thinks again, the dream is still bright and slippery. "Someone I was keeping an eye on."

"Sleeping on the job," he says.

"I was sitting too far back."

"You always do. I can never see you."

"I'm not one of your fans."

"Tell me about it."

She says, softer, "You know what I mean."

He reaches over, rests his hand on her thigh. Her own slides to cover his and as the wind gives their door a gentle shake, she lets herself imagine a boat, warm nights, the two of them learning to sail. They could take provisions and be gone for weeks; it'd solve the problem of separate cities. A moment later he moves to finger the tiny bumps that have swelled along her arms.

"I wish you could be up there with me," he says.

"On stage? You're thinking too small." She wants to suggest

another planet, but instead gets up to turn on the overhead light. "Getting dark out," she says. "Did you notice?"

"I noticed."

She takes careful steps across the carpet. There'd been places that had winked at her before, metallic glints in the shallow pile. She hits the switch and counts three bulbs, watches them bloom.

"So, the next time," he says as she returns. "When will that be?"

The sheet feels cool against her back. "I think I've got a trip to Vancouver in February. Those single-lens fanatics want something woodsy for location."

"You're kidding."

"I know, *woodsy*. Like that'll make it less of a bloodbath. They told me, 'Maybe an ocean cliff, too. For the actors to cling to, then slip.'"

"It's November."

"Yeah. I might be getting too old for this."

"You said next time in February." His voice is thick. "It's only November."

The kids outside start up a coarse drumming, sticks or bars against plastic. The noise is brash and ushering, accompanied by more wind—in the pauses, she hears it push at the branches of trees. "It could be sooner," she says. Then they hear a snap, not a drum beat, but something breaking, and a clatter of metal that's crudely festive.

"Happy New Year," he says.

She pictures the kids scattered, hiding, then peering back over walls or cars to see what'll happen next. The quiet persists. When she hears him breathe in, she drops a foot over the edge of the bed and stretches out a toe, as if it might touch water.

THE SMELL OF NEW rain on asphalt wakes her. She can hear him talking, but his voice is muffled. It doesn't break up the images from her latest dream. They're on that boat, in a cove, and she lounges facing blue sky. Water spots her skin and she brushes at it, annoyed. She can't turn her head to see him fully, but his arm comes into view. He reaches over her, touches the corner of a sail. Then the gesture restarts, the same arm, a glitch.

The air-conditioning snaps on and she tugs up the sheet. Then she remembers, it must be heat, not air—they've met up north this time—and the rain outside is cold.

HIS COLLAPSING WEIGHT DISTURBS the bed. She's lying on her side, facing away from him, and the springs make little waves beneath her.

"The bathroom?" she murmurs, when he nuzzles her hair.

"I was on the phone."

His wife is young and sick, she knows that much. A few months ago, he'd hit pause—explaining it was back to the medical center, in Seattle. "Hold tight," he'd written. "The specialists are swarming. I'll be back when it's under control." His message came in the same email thread they'd been using all morning. *Lost in Malibu*, she'd written as its subject. She waited thirty-one days and then his emails reappeared. She made sure her responses were cheerful and incurious.

The door rattles again, and this time the sound of wind is sharp, close up. She turns to see the closed blinds billow.

"You opened the window," she says.

"It's started." He taps her stomach through the sheet, slowly at first, then faster to indicate a swelling rain. He traces a spiral near her belly button. "Are you cold?"

"I think the heat's on."

"I know," he says, like he can't believe his good fortune. "It's like driving around in a convertible with heated seats."

"What do you know about heated seats?"

"Hey. You think you're the first rich person I've met?"

She turns the rest of the way toward him and presses a

thumb to the middle of his forehead. "That's where the can hit," she says.

"My buddy, my downfall. Did he not like my jokes?"

She nods toward the tattooed ax on his arm, the souvenir she watched him get after the nod from Cannes. "You tried to argue *that* one was a love story."

"Well, a tragedy, too. With expensive scenes. That poor girl's demise, the burning hut. Pyrotechnics don't come cheap."

"You think I didn't see the bill?"

"Though the hero didn't fare any better."

"The infamous beheading."

"He *died* as he lived."

She laughs, draws one of his fingers toward her teeth. "Split in two?" She bites.

"His heart first." He offers her the others, in turn. "Didn't you believe the love?"

"I believed it," she says as the blinds billow again. This time the cold reaches her.

"Sometimes you need blood."

"For love?"

"For life. A lot of fans wanted more."

"A lot of your fans are gore junkies."

"And you're not."

"A junkie?"

"A fan."

"I said I believed the love." She pulls up the sheet and gestures for him to join her. When they're nearly nose-to-nose, she tents it over their heads.

"Do you still?" he asks her.

Her voice drops to a whisper. "You know better than anyone. Nothing good comes at the end."

THE RAIN POUNDS THE roof and splatters the window and door. He stretches to smear the first few drops to have pooled on the sill.

"Hold up," he says, examining his wet fingertips. "How does a *can* cause a heart attack?"

"You lunged at him. Gave it your all."

Her voice catches in a shiver. He raids the closet for a blanket and unfurls it in a theatrical snap. It's dark red and softer than she expects. When he's back beside her, she says, "In my dream you were even bigger. Bearlike. I was sure—"

"*Bigger*?" he says. He flexes his arm and the ax moves. She taps gently on its blade. "Besides, I'm always walking away from those guys. One of them just called my house, and—"

"You didn't walk away." She reaches down, maneuvers her hand between her own legs. His gaze sinks to the slow motion of her arm beneath the covers.

"Is that what you want," he says. "A fighter?"

She bites her lip, shakes her head against the pillow. "Maybe it's the fantasy of being all in."

He strokes the blanket. The light sinks into the rich color. "We could do that," he says.

"Oh, you did. I wish you could have seen yourself—"

"No, here. In real life."

"*This* is real life?" She stops. "My son is nine. *That's* real life."

He frowns and rubs harder at the blanket, jerked motions up and down. Long strands of his dark hair fall forward, grazing his cheeks. The door rattle is constant now, and the wind and rain compete for prominence. She almost doesn't hear him when he says, "She's not dying, you know." He nods toward the bathroom where he'd taken the call. "Right now she's in Albuquerque. Giving a speech called Living with Hodgkin's. That's the disease. Hodgkin's."

She tucks the fallen hair behind his ear, gives him a half smile. "I've never been to Albuquerque."

A strong gust of air lifts the blinds halfway over the bed. He grins wildly and peels the covers down to her knees. The cold air ribbons across her hips and legs. He guides her hand back between her legs and they touch her together, fingers intertwined.

"I was picturing a sailboat," she says. "Up and down the coast."

"Yes! Forget my place or yours."

"You could write scripts from the cabin. Think of all that honeyed light."

"Sharks and little portholes in every draft."

"We'd still be in between."

"It's better than nowhere." He kisses her. "Better than here."

She breathes in sharply as the first drop of rain hits her skin. It sparkles in the light.

"Don't tell me it's not what you want," he says.

With her free hand she wipes the drop from her thigh. "It's what I dream about."

He pushes their hands up hard against her body then, suspending their efforts.

THE BLINDS TWIST AND smack against the wall. One corner of the ceiling has developed a sheen.

"I can't explain how," she says, leaning to bend his foot at the arch. "But at some point, you're gone."

"The dream? You said I didn't die."

"Not dead. At some hospital." She drops the left foot and picks up the right.

"Well, *that's* something."

"But I couldn't get there. There were all these people." She lets go of his foot and raises her arms. "*All these people* in my way."

"They didn't know you cared."

She falls down next to him and he reaches for her necklace, lifts the beads from where they pull across her throat. "You should've been bedside," he says, turning his wrist so the beads form an X.

"They'll never let me in."

"They will. We can get there."

She flips to her back, tugs the beads away, and gestures to the window, the wet ceiling. "We can't even get out of this."

He moves on top, rests on one elbow to wipe at her tears. When she squints past his shoulder, he offers to kill the light, but she shakes her head. "Sharks," she says.

He gives her a puzzled smile, but stays, enters her. She turns her head to face the storm. The blinds are hugging the glass, bent where the window's open to screen. She can already picture the way the thin cords will break, the ends frayed, a piece left to dangle. When the first cord goes, he glances over, but then slips an arm beneath her buttocks, lifts her slightly, and buries his face against her neck. She watches the blinds' right side fall, exposing a wedge of darkness and reflection, a slice of their room distorted in the wet glass.

"Do you think anyone's still out there?" he asks.

"I can't see a thing." She moves and the reflection shifts. She catches a glimpse. "Just us."

"Should we stop?"

She runs her fingers through his hair, then pushes herself gently up against him. Flecks of rain hit the sheets and she closes her eyes against the overhead light. She can still hear the wind, all the rain, and the blinds with slats that continue to waver and bend, jostling to see which can cling the longest before slipping to the thinly carpeted floor.

All Is Not Lost

Alisha Churbe

September 24

Gary Chesterton
468 Lily Valley Road
Grant's Pond, Oregon 99001

Dear Gary,

During my last visit to Darryl's Pit Stop off of Hwy 21, during a particular bout of what my doctor calls EU (excessive urination), and my third or fourth trip to the bathroom that's covered in graffiti, I happened upon your wallet squeezed between the back wall of the toilet and the brick behind it. You're lucky it didn't fall in. For as long as I can remember, or at least the past few months I should say, there hasn't been an actual lid on that toilet. Just a look into the amber glazed insides with all the intricate mechanisms that move when you flush. They get stuck sometimes.

I guess you might not know where your wallet turned up,

it's curious to me that it was in the ladies' room, but maybe you were wasted and didn't realize that's where you'd chosen to unzip your fly and piss away a night's worth of Coors Light. Your keys, or the keys that I can only assume go with the wallet, were on the floor behind the "sanitary napkin" trashcan. The trashcan is never emptied, but in my hurry, I accidentally kicked it trying to get my pants down before pee started down my leg.

I can only imagine how you got home without the keys to your Pontiac and the $23 in cash in your wallet. Your money is safe with me. Although $23 would be a nice bonus for saving your wallet from its toilet water fate, we can discuss it when you retrieve your belongings.

I hope you found your way home. I pray you didn't end up crashing with one of the skanks that frequent this place. If you did, Gary, I really hope you doubled up, or find your way to a clinic soon.

I hope this letter finds you well, Gary. Please write back.

Yours truly,
Marlene Bishop
PO Box 6678
Mulberry, OR 99008

October 14
Dear Gary,

You really must not miss the keys to your house, car, and multiple other houses too much. Got a couple of houses in your name, Gary? Or do you work as a janitor or other service? Seems like you would miss their keys more than you might your own.

I took a further look into your wallet. At first, I looked only to find your name and check how much money was there.

Yesterday, I looked for clues about the kind of guy who might leave his wallet in a ladies' toilet at a small-town bar serving only domestic beers in cans. I don't prefer the beer to be honest, I was never really a drinker.

Beautiful blond boy in your wallet. Must be about 5 in the picture, but I suspect older now as the edges are frayed. The picture looks well worn, well loved. Whoever decided to cut a boy's hair into a bowl cut, anyway? If it was your choice, I don't mean offense. Most parents don't know better. My parents only had girls, so the bowls were reserved for cookie dough and raw meat for meatloaf. We took turns creating new meals, learning how to cook for a man and children one day. A day that is quickly approaching.

I wonder if you've been back to the Pit since you left your wallet. Seems like you'd mention to Glenda that you lost your wallet. I've asked, Gary, and no one has asked her about a lost and/or stolen wallet. Maybe after you lost your wallet, imagining the night you may have had, maybe the next morning you decided you'd never go back. Maybe you've changed your ways. Or maybe it was never who you were to begin with.

All my best, please write back,
Marlene Bishop
PO Box 6678
Mulberry, OR 99008

October 28
Dear Gary,

I have been thinking a lot about fathers and fatherhood. My father is average, nice. He wasn't around much, his work took him out of state often. I guess he'd probably call himself lucky, having three daughters and a wife at home. Can't imagine it being all that peaceful for a man. The sheer number of us meant celebrity magazines, hair accessories, and pots of nail polish pretty much everywhere.

I may have talked with you one night at the Pit. I'm a people person and enjoy a good conversation. You talkative, Gary? My mom tells me the only way to get a husband is to hang out long enough to find one. I don't find many guys, don't get that idea. So many of them have the conversation skills of opossums or are more interested in hitting the mattress than talking about current affairs and the goings on of celebrities. I love to see how they are dressing, their hairdos, and the names of their children. I can't name my kid Pilot or Apple, but I want to find something unique. Nothing biblical, I hate old things. The other thing I can't understand about celebrities, they seem to be always on a diet. I've tried their diets and never lost a pound, maybe I'm not cut out for celebrity life.

I thought I'd found him, Gary, to be honest. You were almost too late. I found him at the Pit of all places. Mitchell asked me to dance one night. We danced at the bar and at his house that night. Sure, he had his problems, mom issues, dad issues, issues with authority. Along with troubles holding down employment or staying in one place for an extended period of time. All he really needed was a woman to love him with all her heart. I was that woman. Gave him my everything, did as my mom told me, found one willing, got pregnant with his kid, Mom said, "No man can walk away from that."

Well, no man but Mitchell. Did you walk away from your son, Gary? Are you the same type of man? Based on the love marked into the photo, I suspect she took him away from you. What kind of woman could take a son from his father? I'm here already months along, supposed to be standing in front of the preacher at the county building in a conspicuously cut dress. Instead, I'm at the Pit four nights a week looking for a new man before it's too late. Kids can be premature, but the ruse is up when you start showing. Slim pickings after that. My mom says, "It doesn't matter, Marly, just find one willing to marry you. The rest will sort itself out later." I'm trying, I really am.

I'm beginning to think I dreamed you up. Are you my guardian angel come to rescue me?

Please write back,
Marlene Bishop
PO Box 6678
Mulberry, OR 99008

November 8
Dear Gary,

Thing is Gary, you seem like a nice man. No woman I can see from the contents of your wallet. There isn't a circular shape worn into the leather, either. It looks like you also had a family who is far away from you now. We could fill the void they left behind.

My friend Crystal says it gets better, men turn into fetish clowns when you're about to pop. That's when you can find yourself a good man, or so she did. Jake loves her pregnant, can't get enough. They are having their fourth. Thing with Jake is he's only attracted to her when she's pregnant, not when her boobs are saggy with milk. I imagine there is a man out there sick enough for that too. No Jake juniors, if you ask me.

Gary, I don't know where you've gone without your things. I sincerely hope that you'll return one day, safe and unharmed. Seems as though a man needs his BiMart membership and his buy 10, get 1 coffee free card to a place called Lottie's. I asked around, no one knows of Lottie's. Must be a small place on the side of the highway. You've only had 4 of your 10 coffees. Seems like you'd be missing that.

Maybe you are on an extended trip to an exotic destination? Without your wallet? You seem to be more of a homebody like me, we are the sort of people who don't do exotic. The sort of people content with the drive-through at the Dairy Queen on a Saturday night as a weekly treat: french fries dipped in a Peanut Buster Parfait. I never understood those people who try new things—what if you don't like it? Seems like a waste.

Your address isn't near, but it isn't far. Forty miles on a good day. Wish now I'd learned to drive, I might have driven to your house and waited outside. Did you meet a tramp at this dive? She steal your things and leave you naked on the side of the road somewhere? You trying to hitchhike your way back?

I've checked the hospitals and the jail, not that I pegged you for that type. You never know where the night will take you and everyone has a bad night sometimes. My bad night was four months ago when I thought the only way to a husband was a roll in the hay and a forgotten pill.

Please write me back.
Yours truly,
Marlene Bishop

November 29, Thanksgiving
Dear Gary,

I've never been to Grant's Pond, though I hear it's nice. Good place to raise kids. I sat at the table with my family and ate too much food today. Guess I am eating for two. Baby wanted three helpings of those succulent yams smothered in toasted marshmallows. It's what makes Thanksgiving, Thanksgiving, don't you think? I make them even though everyone else hates them, I eat most of them and take the rest home for a snack later. Baby also enjoyed the turkey, we took a nap after dinner in Dad's recliner. His job's got him over in Idaho for the entire month. You have to go where the money is.

Is that where you've gone? A job out of state? Did you take off like my sister? My oldest sister, Maggie, hitchhiked out of town about four years ago. With only a backpack, she stuck out her thumb and climbed into the cab of a diesel truck with a complete stranger. We get postcards from her once in a while. She's been everywhere: Albuquerque, Dallas, New Orleans, and Nashville. She never gives a return address and keeps them quite short, "Dear Family, All is well. Enjoying my travels and eating good food. I hope this finds you well. Love and Hugs, Maggie," it's always a variation on the same thing. I don't know if she's found a husband. I seriously doubt she has any kids.

I have three sisters and none are like me. My youngest sister, Meghan, married the first boy she ever met. Jesse is a local kid, he's just always been here. They met at 15 and married two days after my sister turned 18. She was already pregnant with Amy.

My second sister, Misty, left town. She applied for scholarships and actually got one. She went to college in Portland, met Aaron, and they live together there now. She says she's not ready or in any hurry for marriage and she's undecided about children. I don't know what she's waiting for. When we talk she says she feels sorry for me and baby, wished I would have sorted things out better. Wish I had, too. She said I can come and visit in such a quiet and reserved way, as if she really doesn't mean it.

Do you pick up your mail or is a neighbor sorting through it in your absence? You keep getting letters from a woman. God knows what your neighbor must think. Where could you be? I imagine Grant's Pond to have nice suburban homes in neighborhoods where everyone knows each other and the kids can walk to school. Houses have central air, dishwashers, and double car garages. I don't cook as well as my sisters, I get stuck with the dishes after each meal. I dream of a dishwasher. Front lawns are perfectly flat and trimmed, all the men mow them on the weekends before the evening bbqs. Hamburgers, mostly, sometimes steaks—never those hot dogs in cellophane packaged for 99 cents at the canned food outlet.

Please write as soon as you are able.
Yours truly,
Marlene Bishop

December 11
Dear Gary,

The weirdest thing happened to me today. I actually felt the baby. I hadn't felt him before. I've been rubbing my belly hoping to wake the little booger from his sleep, but he didn't come to, until today. I think about the baby every day. Between you and me, I'm scared. My sister, Meghan, has told me all the gory details of her childbirth and first years with Amy. I honestly believe she doesn't have much fun. She had a rough birth and further complications after the baby arrived. She's healthier now, but it was a very slow recovery. What if something happens to me Gary? Who will take care of my kid?

I've been thinking of names for the baby. They asked me if I wanted to know the sex and I've decided to leave it as a surprise. Makes it a little more fun that way. I think I will name her Rain, if it's a girl. It's sort of catchy and definitely not an old name. Rain because I swear that is the only thing it's been doing for as far back as I can remember this year, though it's been bitter cold at night. Should see snow any day, but I won't name her Snow. No daughter of mine will be waiting in a poisoned apple induced coma for a magic kiss. My mother wants me to name her Kathleen, but it's not my style.

I hope she meets a guy someday like I imagine you to be. I

also hope she doesn't take her child away from that nice man. I hope she doesn't hold it against me that I tried to find her a good father, but failed. Maybe there's still time, Gary. Maybe I can make it up to her one day.

Truly,
Marlene Bishop

December 24, Christmas Eve
Dear Gary,

It's Christmas, my favorite holiday. All the candy, cookies, eggnog, brown sugar baked ham, the lights, and all the fun carols. Me and baby have been "Rockin' Around the Christmas Tree" since December 1st, when the local radio finally plays the Christmas tunes. I think they should play them all year round, slip them in every once in a while, who doesn't love them? And they always make me want to boogie. Boogying is getting a little bit harder these days, it looks more like a sway, but we are doing it.

I got to see the baby again this week. They took more pictures of him today, using an ultrasonic? I can't remember what they called it. He actually looks like a baby now. They've tried to convince me that the blobs circled on the screen and later in the prints was a baby. I don't think they were looking in the right place until today. The baby seems to look a lot like his dad. Very thin, tall, an egg-shaped head that never quite looked like it fit.

Today, he's awake and kicking. He must enjoy the blinking lights and all the singing. Misty made a rare appearance this year. She says she's worried about me. My sisters (less Maggie) and I have been singing and dancing our way through the food preparation since Monday. I'm sure I told you that I am not a very good cook. I think I am, but my sisters do not. I always get put in charge of setting the table and washing the dishes. My sisters do a lot of work, but I contribute in my own way.

I hope the baby likes the food I cook. Meghan has made it so Amy is so picky. Meghan makes a number of dinners each night. One for Amy, usually chicken nuggets and ketchup, along with a box of Hamburger Helper for Jesse. Some nights she has a few bites of each because she doesn't have the energy to cook something she might like eating. I plan to make one dinner and we'll all enjoy it.

Truly,
Marlene Bishop

January 4
Dearest Gary,

I am beginning to think this whole "find a man, get pregnant" thing isn't as great as I thought it would be. I have failed at it. I thought it would be different, I thought I'd be married with a small gold band on my ring finger, a husband to cook for, who would rub my always swollen feet and say nice things to my enormous belly for the baby to hear. I imagined picking out baby clothes together, deciding between frogs or giraffes for the baby's room. Instead, my sister dropped off a box of hand-me-down clothes. Leftovers from my niece. Cute kid, but a little bit creepy. She's very quiet and stares with serious intent.

I hope my kid is more playful and happy. I read that babies pick up on your mood when you are pregnant and it can actually define your kid's personality. I've been trying to stay happy and hopeful, so baby gets the best start she can under these circumstances. The plan worked for my mother, she and dad have been together forty years. Guess the secret could be that Dad is absent most of the time.

I am unsure of what to tell my kid. I really don't know what the best plan or strategy is. Guess my strategy was a failure. I don't think I am where I'm supposed to be.

Are you where you are supposed to be?

Yours truly,
Marlene

January 28
Dear Gary,

I hope you don't find this too forward, but I want to name him Gary, if it's a boy. I'm not adding "junior" because he isn't really, is he? You can't be a junior without a father. I've been looking for a newer name, but nothing fancy or weird. I considered Trevor, but I think Gary will be a better fit.

I tried it out over the past few days and baby seems to like it. He moves and kicks a lot these days. I rub my stomach, "Hush, Gary, everything is okay." Doctor told me to walk if I ever want this baby to come. So, I've been taking walks through the neighborhood on nice days, past the school where I went and where Gary will go, the park with the brand new jungle gym.

When I was a kid, it only had a swing set and a merry-go-round. Didn't matter, we spent hours having so much fun in that park. We talked about how great our lives were going to be and how handsome our husbands would be. It would get to dusk, a surreal light of day, red sky sunsets. Rules were we had to be home by the time the streetlights came on. We'd hear them start to buzz, then we'd run like hell. We'd arrive panting and worn out.

Mom would give us plastic cups of Kool-Aid and graham cracker sandwiches with frosting centers. Strawberry was my favorite, but I also liked chocolate. Mom always gave us dessert before dinner, it was our own little tradition. Meant we'd get dessert before Dad called at 7 each night. We'd all take turns telling him goodnight and receiving his long distance hugs and kisses before bedtime.

It's too bad my kid won't get any 7 p.m. calls. I'm scared to have a boy. I don't know what boys do or how boys are. He'll need advice I can't give him. I hope he doesn't turn out hating me for this. I'll tell him to find a nice girl and not walk away from his child.

Yours truly,
Marlene

February 12
Dearest Gary,

I really wish I could know where you've gone. You are such a mystery and I have spent many fitful nights caught up in dreams of all the horrible mishaps you may have encountered. I am haunted by all the terrible things that may have happened to you, but hopeful that things have turned out better for you in some way. I spent your $23 on a stuffed animal for the baby, I think he or she will really like the panda I picked out. I hope you don't mind.

Sitting is restricting the baby too much, he needs room to move. It's February and snow is falling outside, so I don't know how I am supposed to get walks in. Glenda told me I should go to South Shore Shopping Center and do laps. I don't know why they call it South Shore, there isn't a beach around, but I have been walking and shopping and daydreaming. Yesterday, I got really tired halfway through the first lap and collapsed into an easy chair outside the cinnamon roll place. I ordered one, I couldn't help it, they smell so good and the baby likes them. I think she'll be like me, at least I hope so. But maybe not too much, I hope my kid makes better decisions than I did.

The cinnamon rolls are near the kids' play center. While I sat picking apart the stickyroll with gooey frosting, I watched the kids playing. There was a group of girls playing with a large gray castle. One had a horse, another is holding a princess. Damsels in distress and knights in shining armor, fairy tales. There was a group of boys throwing beanbags at each other and carrying bow and arrows. They were in the Sherwood Forest in a battle. Robin Hood, Maid Marian, and Little John. The sound of laughter and play. The kids were having such a fun time in their imaginary land.

I saw moms watching their kids. They were surrounded by brightly colored plastic containers and juice boxes, many of them sitting half crumpled. Squished by little hands to get the juice from the bottom. Some of the moms were also nursing and caring for smaller infants, swaddled in cloth to protect them from the world outside. I am scared at the thought of one kid, I can't imagine caring for two. These mini people need their mothers right now. Just like mine will need me.

Gary, I watched and there were very few dads. Some kept watch for a time so their wives could quickly look in a nearby store. Others broke the news to their kid that it was time to go. I watched a dad wipe tears from his daughter's face. He was trying to be so nice, but there is only so much time you can stay in a make-believe land before you have to go back to real life.

If these women can do it, I think I might also be able to do it. Gary, my mom might be right, I may have imagined you. It's about time I stopped writing you and let you get on with your life, the same as I plan to do.

I hope this letter one day finds you well.

All my best,
Marlene

The Promised Land

Jan Baross

BAKERSFIELD, CALIFORNIA, 1948.

Father's black hair was wild in the wind as our Chevy made its gradual descent into the stifling San Joaquin Valley. We were headed for redneck central. Bakersfield, California, a small outpost of primitive politics, hot flat aggressive agriculture, and oil when oil was plentiful. Father had found a job in spite of his being Jewish.

Uprooted from the cool breezes of San Francisco Bay, our overheated car steamed protest all the way through the burlap colored Tehachapis. Ahead of us lay a dry landscape of biblical proportion. The width of the great valley was split by a black spine of highway or the mirage of a highway that wavered in the breathless heat. It was a place the wisest passed through, but we were staying.

Sweat ran down Father's face as he clung tightly to the wheel. The threat of death by Cossacks had propelled him out of a Russian ghetto. His immigrant answer to the future was to become a gladly overworked knight of commerce. He thought a paycheck would insulate his family.

Mother understood better than any of us what lay ahead.

A woman of big-city possibilities she had endured a child-hood indentured to small-town sensibilities. And now Father was returning her to the same insular life. When her good-natured papa was run over as he stepped off a Memphis summer streetcar, his senseless death formed and deformed within her a volcanic impatience not to waste time.

"Look out the window, children," she said as we sped along Highway 99. There were vast tracts of dusty fields and palms on either side. We were drowsy with the heat but we took our vigil at the window. "Remember those trees," she said. "You may never see them again."

Her road-trip mantra, "You may never see them again," always set a terror ticking in me. How was I to gather all those images ghosting past? I looked to the dry distant mountains surrounding San Joaquin Valley. They did not move and would not crumble in memory after my five-year-old eyes left them behind.

The car sped past the outskirts of Bakersfield, past motels spread like tiny refugee camps. An occasional dust-covered eucalyptus drooped in a loose welcome, dead leaves spiraling in our wake. Through open windows wind blew in the desert, the grit of my childhood mixed with the smell of the highway.

In those days there were no seatbelts. I rolled across the back seat of the car for a tired assault on damp little brother, taking pleasure in his quiet gasp as I pinched a pudgy thigh. The blond prince bit his lip to keep silent not wanting to get me in trouble. I resented his loyalty almost as much as I resented his birth.

Mother glanced back at our silent truce, her eyes unfocused, and then turned away. Her thoughts would never find purchase on the monochrome horizon. It was too far from her dream of circumambulating the *arrondissements* of Paris. She dreamt in symphonic uplifts; a glass apartment against a Paris sky, ascending plumes of lathered espresso, steaming crepes served in outdoor cafes where, even in the recent rubble of war, every cobblestone was an upended shrine.

"We will stay for a year," Father had promised. Just until he could pull together a passable nest egg to sustain our exodus back to The Bay. The orbit of one year, he said. Mother marked the date on a small calendar she carried in her purse. One unbearable year that turned into twenty-five by the time Mother buried Father and left on Air France.

Welcome to Bakersfield. Our Chevy sped past the sign: Population: 40,462.

Mother pulled on the large straw hat that hid her ivory skin. She would wear that hat whenever she wanted to remind Father of his exodus promise. Over the next quarter century we would hear her say with growing alarm, and less and less humor, "Daddy, whenever you're ready."

Her only fond memory of Bakersfield, she wrote years later on Hotel Eiffel stationary, was the seductively warm nights when she stood in the backyard garden without a shawl and felt embraced by a golden Manet heat. She still smoked then and held the cigarette French style in her fingers. As the dusk fell, she would snub out her last cigarette in the barbecue ash. She returned to us from the dark, smelling of smoke, and pulled on her sweater in the cryogenic chill of our air-conditioned home.

"Oh God," said Mother, "Are we really here?"

Bakersfield was written in huge weathered blue letters above our heads, a yellow sky bridge spanning the highway. Mother's own personal diaspora had begun. She looked and could not look away. She was now an official exile in the vast Mojave.

I shielded my eyes from the excruciating glare of plate-glass windows. The Nile, a baroque movie house, contrasted with the board game sameness of the other buildings. The main street of Chester Avenue seemed wide enough to sail a royal barge over the wavy heat of asphalt.

We were lost as Father wound us through one dried-out

neighborhood after another. Tumbleweeds clung to sagging cy-clone fences along the dusty roads and dogs with long tongues lay collapsed in the sparse shade.

When we stopped on the corner of one potholed street, Mother checked the address and moaned. Father sighed an apology.

The Chevy's overheated engine got us up the sloping drive-way of a small brick house painted white with a black wooden door. The roof was covered in red Spanish tiles.

"Oh, good, now we're Mexicans," said Mother.

Father, a man of endless gratitude, beamed at the first home he actually owned. He believed Mother would adapt, that we all would.

The car had become a four-wheeled toaster oven. Little brother and I tumbled out in our sweaty cotton sunsuits. The cement driveway burnt through our thin-soled leather sandals. How could anyone even dress for such a place?

Mother held the key as though she were skewering the front door. To enter the house we had to step up on a cement block that was not attached to the house. The wood door opened easily, sun beaten and peeling. The gap at the base might ensure a breeze.

Inside the thick walls it was cool but stuffy. Father opened the windows and left the door wide. The four of us stood in the middle of the empty front room, whitewashed brick walls and a stone fireplace. The polished cement floor was painted a glossy red as though it had recently been hosed down with an open artery.

Mother put her damp fingers on our shoulders and drew us close as though we were in danger. We shifted as close as possi-ble, which made our eight-legged isolation seem more vulner-able in the vast room, a family of bowling pins anticipating the strike.

"Children," Mother whispered, "don't tell anyone you're Jewish. No one. Understood?"

We nodded. Even little brother at four had been inoculated with our parents' fear. The Holocaust ending not that long before I was born. We knew we could have easily been executed in another place for being the same people who stood in the middle of this crimson floor.

There was a knock at the door. We all startled and turned as if attached to the same thought.

A postman in a blue cap made a kind of salute with a letter in his hand. His tan face and thick arms were saturated with soft wrinkles.

"You the new Jewish doc, Doc?" the postman said.

Mother's nails sunk into my shoulder. I held my breath. Little brother reached for my hand, his curly blond hair trembled. Father said nothing, nodded slightly, trying his gracious best to comply and deny.

The postman stepped up onto the cement block and leaned into the house. Father reached out to take the letter.

The postman said, "Welcome to Bakersfield, folks."

He walked down the cement driveway whistling, turning past an old fig tree.

Father looked at the letter. His own father had deliberately scoured the ghetto syllables. He read our name slowly as though it were foreign to him.

"Does that sound Jewish to you?" he asked, looking up at us.

The air out of mother's lungs was a punctured tire. She walked to the door shielding her eyes against the Bakersfield sun.

"One year, Daddy," she said.

The World, the Flesh, and the Devil

Christi Krug

"MY CHILDREN DO NOT participate in the idolatry of Santa Claus," said the man squeezed into a student chair at the front of my classroom, his kneecaps jammed under the desk, legs splayed at sharp angles. The bottom corners of his gray merino sport coat stuck out.

The misfitted image unsettled me. I felt like one of his kids—the two most timid in my class. I hooked my high heels on the cross bar of my stool for support.

"That's very discerning of you." My voice was fluffy and artificial in my ears, like pink feathers. I straightened, trying to recover a sense of authority. "I encourage children to come up with their own fantasies." I flinched: *wrong word.* "What I mean is—"

"At my house, I don't encourage fantasies of any kind," said Mr. Mayhew.

I nodded, and the sharp point of my brooch poked through my sweater to flesh. Mr. Mayhew had a lot of influence at Home

First Education Center. I wondered if he'd had something to do with my little chat with the principal some weeks back. But for now, what filled my vision was the shine of his mink eyes, the planes of his youthful face. I swallowed, resting my hands in a hammock of skirt.

Behind black rims, the mink eyes stared unblinking. "*Mrs.* Kalani," he said, while I shivered at the small word in his mouth. I was teaching the children to say *Ms.* but it was slow going; they'd never known a *Ms.* "Such things are a threat to faith."

When I was eleven, I tore my Luke Skywalker poster into bits because the visiting preacher told us *Star Wars* was Satanic. At thirteen, I hunkered alone on Halloween night in an unlit house, listening to a radio preacher list the head-rolling, blood-boiling, devil-worshipping implications of October 31. At twenty, I married without having gone on a single date, thus avoiding that enemy, the world. "I understand about threats," I said.

But if he knew the facts, there was no way he would want me teaching his little girl and boy. My first act of defiance had been keeping the tithe of one month's salary, one year ago. My husband, Patrick, went through the roof. That was the beginning of the end.

My daughter, Sarah, was trying to make sense of it.

Mommy, how come you don't go to church anymore?

Daddy says if you went to church, we could all live together again.

Mr. Mayhew shelved his chin on a folded hand. His shoulders were strong right angles, from an era when self-examination was not necessary. Farmers worked their land; wives their kitchens. A man paid the bills, protecting you from the world. So you could take care of your child.

The only thing that mattered now was Sarah.

Mr. Mayhew shook his head, sending movement through sleek brown hair. He resettled on his hand. "Explain what you mean by fantasies."

Steam from microwave macaroni and cheese was wafting

from the next door lunch room, tickling my dry throat. "No fantasies. I encourage—imaginativeness is all."

There were footsteps, chatter, and the scrape of chairs as students filed out of the classrooms into the arms of their parents. Mr. Mayhew glanced at the clock. Light from the window showed a hint of beard. It might be soft, then again, bristly. Patrick never could grow a beard.

"I want to see their schoolwork," he said carefully and a little loudly, the way people do when you don't speak their language. "But you need to understand my priorities. My wife and I are bringing up our children to believe the Truth. No fairy tales. No fabrications."

I shuffled through wrinkled papers.

"And this Christmas, I will not tolerate the mention of Santa Claus."

Finding what I was looking for, I thrust at him Ruth Mayhew's story, "A Day at the Zoo."

"Today we will take a trip," announsed Papa. And presently they all went to the zoo. "The girafs are so tall!" exclaimed Henry. "Would you like an ice cream?" declared Mama kindly. And they all had ice cream. "I'm scared of the snake!" Polly cried angshusly. "That is because he is the most subtil of all the animals that God created," said Papa wisely. Soon it was time to hurry home so they didn't miss their Bible reading time. "Thank you for taking us to the zoo," said Polly and Henry together.

Luke Mayhew had written about his father's stamp collection, and the most remarkable thing was his handwriting at eleven: hard and infantile, in pencil so dark that the paper was pocked with tiny holes.

"Your children are very good writers." I could now add lying to my sins.

Mr. Mayhew's expression did not change. He spread the

papers on the desktop, smoothing them flat. The rustling of his
clothes lifted the scents of clover and rain.

I wondered, did he and his wife *enjoy* sex? Was that allowed
in his denomination?

A muscle tensed along Mr. Mayhew's lean, tanned jaw. I
stood and walked to the white board. I wiped a clearing in the
crowded ink with the flat of my fist. I wrote: *Imagination is more
important than knowledge. — Einstein.*

"God's gift to us," I said.

Of course I was really talking about sex.

There was a drop of moisture on Mr. Mayhew's pale bottom
lip, just above his perfect chin. For a moment I felt the dread of
sitting in church, convinced the preacher could read my mind.
I tugged down my skimpy pink angora sweater.

For sure, this man saw me as a lost, worldly woman. He
saw me as clueless.

How could I explain this wasn't the whole picture? All my
life, I'd followed the rules. I had taught Sunday School classes
that rivaled any sermon.

"Without imagination, we wouldn't be able to create any
kind of life for our children," I said, my voice getting stronger.
"How could we teach them to believe in the future?" Even if that
future meant divorced parents. Living on Top Ramen. Having a
mother who was no longer accepted in church. "How could we
show our children how to give, to imagine God's blessings, to
hope for miracles?"

He stared, nostrils narrowed.

The principal had been similarly unimpressed with my
philosophies. *A few parents have voiced concern over the books you
are reading to your class.* He'd nodded, ample paunch hidden
by his enormous oak desk. He formed the words with mobile,
chunky lips. *Remember the population we serve. You must respect
their beliefs.*

Oh, but I *was* careful. In Creative Writing, I used the term "far-fetched stories," avoiding the taboos of fairies, witches, and ghosts in this rural, religious community. Homeschooling parents came to the Home First Education Center to supplement their children's education, not threaten it with unwelcome ideas.

Patrick, too, was careful about evil influences. Two Christmases ago he had begun a routine inspection of my library books. "Looks Satanic," he murmured over a stack of Grimms' tales.

Daddy doesn't like this story. He gets scared. But not me, Mommy, keep reading!

There was no telling how many students had their reading monitored, line by line, *Left Behind* books notwithstanding. Through the months working here, I watched their faces flash, then their pencils. Benjamin wrote, "The Princess And The Frozen Peas." Luke worked all night, skipping his hour of Disney Channel to finish "Dragon and Ailien," and even silent Martha wrote about a friendly giant. But nothing could penetrate the wooden complaisance of Ruth and Luke Mayhew.

One day I dropped the word "magic."

Ruth Mayhew's brow puckered as she gripped her desk, the only time she forgot to raise her hand. *We're not supposed to talk about that,* she whispered. Across the aisle, Luke just looked at me, torso straight and tall, pencil hovering over a blank white page.

"Let me ask you something," Mr. Mayhew said, placing one long-fingered hand atop the other on the laminate desktop. He leaned forward. "Are you a believer?"

Rebellious, lustful, confused, alone. "Yes," I said. "I grew up attending church not far from here." No sex for thirteen months. No arms like yours, muscled and swept with small dark curls, to encircle the small of my back.

"What I mean is," he said, "are you born again?"

"Yes," I said. "I was eleven years old." Or seven. Or thirty.

Or maybe I was born again this morning, on my walk, when I watched the swans through the reeds and cottonwoods as they splashed in the creek where they return every December.

"Then surely you understand where I'm coming from."

Understand, yes. I nodded. But I can never go back.

"I'm glad we had this talk." He unfolded from the chair bit by bit like a praying mantis.

As he offered his hand, I stepped forward to take it, feeling the prick in my chest. The brooch I was wearing: it was a Santa. Mr. Mayhew shook my hand weakly, avoiding the sweat collecting below my fingers. I'd have to get to the preschool in a hurry. It was my weekend to have Sarah.

I was taking her to Santa's workshop, so she could sit on his lap, and tell him what she wished for.

The Dog War

Ellen Davidson Levine

IF YOU WANT MY opinion—and as my wife Sally says, you may not—to understand the Dog War you have to go back to the mid-twentieth century, when the Legal Family homestead was subdivided. The Legals kept a few acres and sold the rest to folks like Sally's family, the Chesleys, and to the Walkers, the Oldhams, and a few more.

They came to Oregon from the Midwest, most of them, solid, hardworking people who voted for Eisenhower because he was a war hero and he looked like their uncle. They built respectable ranch-style homes, put in gardens, kept chickens for the eggs, and ran a few head of cattle on their acreage. They drove Ford pickups. The men worked in the woods or at one of the mills. Backbreaking, dirty work but good money. The women stayed home, tended the animals, the garden, the house and the kids, and worked as hard as any man pulling green chain.

Things were still like that when Sally and I married. We rented an apartment in town, two blocks from the high school where I spent my entire career trying to convince teenagers that history matters. When Sally's parents died, her mother from cancer, her dad from loneliness, we moved into the Legal Creek house. Some people still call it the Chesley place, although my name's Jim Shuster and that's been the name on the tax roll for years. I'm still an outsider after all this time.

Maybe that's why I liked the so-called hippies and longhairs when they came. Some bought cheap parcels of land and put up an A-frame, log cabin, or even a teepee—housing some old-timers thought wasn't a real house compared to a three bedroom, two bath with attached garage. The old-timers dismissed hippies as druggies and fools. Didn't help when there were characters like Duke, from Miner's Gulch. He was a bad one.

Which is not to say there wasn't weirdness and wrongness on the old-timers' side. Like Old Oldham and his wife, Ellie, who dyed her hair bright red well into her eighties, prune-faced Twyla Walker and her dull-witted husband Jack, and the Legals, Laurence and Verlie. Laurence was the only true Legal Creek old-timer. Like his father before him, he'd lived in the Legal farmhouse since the day he was born. Verlie was next, having moved here when she married Laurence, before he shipped out to the Philippines in World War II.

The six of them were particularly cranky about the hippies moving onto Legal Creek, although who do you think was guilty of selling off five-acre parcels to those kids? On Sundays, the Legals, Oldhams, and Walkers would stand in the church parking lot after the service and complain to each other about wobbly houses, weedy gardens and loose dogs and especially the hippies who lived at the Monte Verde commune, which shared a disputed property line with the Legals.

The commune was founded in the mid-1970s by college dropouts from places like Indiana and Iowa, Montana and Wisconsin. Nice, smart kids. Since Sally and I had visited the commune and Laurence Legal hadn't, I argued with him one Sunday when I overheard him say Monte Verde was home to drug-crazed hippies from San Francisco.

"They're dirty and their dogs all have worms," he added. "Their kids too."

"Damn it, Laurence," I said, having reached the limit of my own tolerance. "That's an ignorant, hateful thing to say."

"You can't talk to Laurence that way," Verlie scolded. "You're not being very Christian. And on a Sunday too."

I thought that was ironically funny, but when I shared the joke with Pastor Carson, mentioning no names of course, he frowned and cleared his throat and asked if I didn't think those hippies were dragging society's morals down and maybe something should be done about them. I stopped going to church then. Sally still goes, sometimes.

Now that I'm retired, I do my worshipping when Bear and I take our daily constitutional. Walk up the road and I see the slopes of Blue Mountain. Coming down, I get a panoramic view of the Siskiyous. Bear is a black Lab we named for how he looked as a pup. That was a while back. These days, Bear is slowed by arthritis. Me too. We still enjoy the walk. Fact is, except for Sally and the kids, I prefer his company.

Cats are another story. Sally's allergic, so we've never had indoor cats. I've always kept one or two down at the barn to scare off mice and whatever else. The cats are overflow from Chip and Barb Buford's place. By now, there's probably as many cats roaming the Buford place as there are pieces of junk, including corroded skeletons of cars, trucks, even a bus. The current cat living in the barn I call Chester, because he limps. If you're too young to have watched *Gunsmoke* on TV back in the day, then you won't get it. Chester is gray with a ragged tail, a scar over one eye, and a patchwork of missing fur. He's feisty and he's lasted longer than most of the barn cats. One thing about Chester, he appreciates the scraps I leave for him. He says thanks by rubbing against my legs, purring like a well-oiled engine. Most cats seem ungrateful and haughty, always jumping on laps where they're not wanted. Sally has to take a double dose of allergy medicine if we visit what we privately call "a cat house."

It was a cat named Susie that launched the Dog War. Susie's a ridiculous name for a cat, especially a pedigree Persian, but there you have it. Susie belonged to the Ayreses, who'd bought a ten-acre parcel from the Oldhams in the early 1980s. The Ayreses built a big hodge-podge of a house with small windows, as if they didn't care to look at the breathtaking view. The house sits back near the tree line with a long paved driveway sweeping up to a four-car garage.

The Ayreses had two girls, Cinnamon and Ginger. Both names would've been better for a cat. Another thing, the Ayreses didn't have a dog. Crazy to be living in the country with a namby-pamby feline, no dog, and probably not a gun or rifle anywhere. I'm no John Wayne, but I can tell you story after story about having to shoot a porcupine in the front yard or unwanted critters considering residence under the house.

Melanie Ayres came home one day to find Susie's bloody, beat-up corpse in the middle of the driveway. Given the speed and erratic nature of Melanie's driving, I've always wondered if she ran it over with her big white van. It's a suspicion I've kept private, strongly encouraged to do so by Sally. Sally says I have too many opinions. That may well be. I hope I practice what I taught—to be rational and fair and to consider all the facts, not just the ones I prefer.

Melanie immediately concluded the cat had been maimed and murdered by a dog. Not just any dog but a dog named Romeo, a great galumph of a mutt that lived at the top of the road, about a mile after the pavement ends. Romeo was guilty of impregnating more than one female dog in the vicinity, including Dick Root's prize sheepdog. But he—Romeo, not Dick—was a gentle soul and less capable of murdering a cat than my old Bear. That didn't stop Melanie Ayres from calling the sheriff and the county animal control and about half the

neighbors on the road to demand that something be done about
Romeo the cat killer.

The problem was Romeo belonged to the Murphys, a care-
less couple with a herd of tow-headed kids about nine months
apart in age. Katie Murphy was nice enough and a good mother, keeping the children clean and well-behaved. Her husband
Tim was another story altogether. I'd been up to the Murphys'
cabin a couple times, once to return Romeo when he wandered
down to my place and another when I saw pregnant Katie and
a couple kids hitchhiking. Of course, I gave them a ride. Both
times, I was treated to the sight of a dazed-looking Tim, wearing logger boots, boxer shorts, and an untied bathrobe.

It goes without saying that the sheriff wouldn't investigate
a cat death, even a brutal one. The animal control people were
busy in Sam's Valley dealing with rabid skunks. So Melanie
Ayres decided to take the law into her own hands. As the story
goes, at least the version I got from Sally who got it from Verlie
Legal, Melanie threw the mutilated cat in the van and raced up
the road to the Murphys' shack. She honked the horn until Tim
emerged wearing his boots and robe outfit. That sight must've
sent Melanie over the edge. She got out of the van, cradling the
bloody cat corpse and screaming at Tim about his killer dog.

That's when Romeo came bounding at Melanie with a tail
wagging, tongue slurping welcome. I can picture the scene—
Melanie shrieking like all get-out, the dog thinking it's a game,
jumping and barking like crazy, Tim Murphy standing on the
porch in his underwear and untied robe, a puzzled expression
on his face. Melanie got so frustrated, she took the dead cat and
pitched it at Tim. Hit his forehead dead-center and knocked
him down. Melanie ran back to her car and drove off in a swirl
of dust and gravel, wailing and weeping and driving so crazily
she about crashed into Christopher Legal, great-grandnephew
of Laurence and Verlie. Back then, before he started working
for the bank, Christopher drove a red Porsche, a car so bright

and shiny and noisy that you'd think anyone could see it and hear it from a long way off. From what I heard, Melanie never noticed a thing.

That afternoon, when Cinnamon and Ginger got home from school, they were outraged at Melanie for abandoning the beloved Susie's corpse. Melanie decided she was a terrible mother for denying her daughters a proper burial of the cat because without this, they would never get closure. I think I know what that means and it's crap. When our dachshund puppy was carried off by an owl, my kids held a memorial ceremony. Sarah read a poem she wrote for the occasion and Jeff played "Puff the Magic Dragon" on the guitar he got for his birthday. The kids got plenty of closure, corpse or no corpse.

Melanie got back in her van and drove to the Murphy place for the second time that day. This time Katie came to the door, arms crossed and a mean look in her eyes. Or so I imagine. Katie had plenty of spunk and why she put up with that husband of hers I'll never know. She certainly didn't take kindly to Melanie Ayres' screaming. Katie calmly informed Melanie the dead cat's body was in the garbage with the dirty diapers and if Melanie wanted it she could feel free. Melanie actually retrieved the cat's body and brought it home for the funeral.

Sally and I took the kids to Portland that year, to spend the holidays with my folks. New Year's Day, the state got hit by a snowstorm that dumped a couple feet or more of snow, followed by a thaw that melted everything in a hurry. All over Oregon, creeks and rivers were at flood stage. We opted to stay put until the weather calmed down. We didn't get home until January fourth.

Aside from an oak that fell near the barn, a tree I'd intended to bring down anyway, we got through the bad weather just fine. Some of our neighbors weren't so lucky. And as history shows, bad luck can lead to blame and blame becomes a line drawn in the sand.

Some of the worst damage was at the Legal place where the creek crested its banks. There was floodwater up to the doorstep of the old farmhouse, first time in anyone's memory. Receding water took the woodshed, a number of Verlie's prize rose bushes, and the entire front lawn.

We were all just recovering from the storms and the flooding and the feeling of vulnerability that a natural disaster stirs up when we started hearing about missing dogs. First to disappear was Finnegan, a beautiful but dumb Irish setter belonging to Jason Cohn, not technically a Legal Creeker since he lives over the hill on Misery Flats. That happened sometime the second week in January. Over the next few weeks, a series of small yappy dogs disappeared. Then it got worse. Almost every day a dog vanished, leaving no trace. There were flyers advertising missing dogs on every telephone pole up and down Legal Creek Road and on the bulletin board at the market. Meanwhile, we tried to keep our dogs inside as much as possible. But at some point, a dog has to go out.

Back then, we had Poet, a Lab mix, smart but a bit too friendly. Sure enough, I let him out one night in May, called for him five minutes later, but he didn't come back. That night and weeks after, I searched without finding a sign of him. Still miss that damn dog, even though I've got another perfectly good one hanging around.

By summertime, it got so people had lost two and three dogs—the first dog and then its replacements—one after another. Some people kept dogs on leash even for a poop run in the middle of the night. Didn't seem to discourage the dognapper.

For me, it wasn't just the missing dogs. I worried about the accusations that were traded back and forth. Old-timers accused the commune of stealing the dogs. Monte Verde folks, who'd also suffered dognappings, were equally convinced it was an old-timers' campaign of harassment to drive them away. Now, Sally and I have always stayed neutral in most matters involving neighbors. Not Switzerland neutral, which is prof-it-driven diplomacy in my opinion, but neutral because we find most of the disputes to be silly and not worth getting excited about. Over the years, we'd stayed amiable with the Legals and the Oldhams and the others. They regarded Sally as an old-timer and therefore tolerated me. We'd also gotten to know some of the newcomers and every summer, hired a few of the Monte Verde kids to help Sally weed the garden and keep up the yard.

The Dog War made it impossible to remain impartial, especially after Melanie Ayres told Verlie she'd seen hippies sneaking up the Legal driveway the very night, back in late January, when the Legal dog went missing. I'd seen the Legals' flyer tacked to trees and telephone poles, with a full-page color photo of their wrinkle-faced shar-pei, unforgettably named Winkle. Melanie's phone call ignited Laurence and Verlie. They began a campaign against the commune.

It was my opinion Melanie saw nothing. I told Laurence so when he came over to recruit me to the battle. In retrospect, my tone of voice may have been a touch arrogant.

"For one thing," I told him, "why'd she wait six months to speak up? For another, your driveway winds alongside the creek and is pretty much hidden behind a tangle of blackberry vines. Plus, it was nighttime. Given the blackberries and the darkness, how'd she see anything?" I lifted a fourth finger. "And, she was probably driving too fast in her big white van. Add to all that the fact that Melanie is a troublemaker." I held up my hand, all five digits extended. Then I made a fist. "Case closed."

We were sitting at the kitchen table, drinking coffee. Setting the mug down with a loud thump, Laurence scraped his chair away from the table. He stood, looked down at me, shook his head. "You'll be sorry, Jim," he said, "now you're one of them." He had declared war and I was an enemy collaborator. I wasn't sure whether to laugh or worry about his vague threat. I knew

Laurence had always been suspicious of me as a city boy from Portland and a school teacher to boot. But he'd never been openly hostile.

The same week Laurence and I had our confrontation, Sally brought home a year-old black Lab. She'd stopped at the market after work and there was a woman in the parking lot with a cute dog and a sad story. Sally is a sucker for both. The minute the kids saw the cuddly Lab there was no question he was staying. We named him Bear.

It was Bear who solved the dognapping mystery.

That first night, we bedded Bear on blankets in the service porch. We wrapped an alarm clock in a towel, so the steady tick-tock would comfort him in his new surroundings. Damn dog commenced to whimper and squeal for what seemed like hours. Every time I dozed off, he'd start up again. Everyone else slept soundly through the ruckus. I got up several times to hush him and finally gave up. I put on a lightweight jacket, grabbed a leash, and clipped it on the dog's collar. He shut up as soon as we were outside.

Suddenly, I didn't mind being rousted from my warm bed. It was the edge of dawn, that time between dark and light when everything seems to be holding its breath, waiting. The air smelled of lilacs and there was a faint, not unpleasant whiff of skunk or maybe fox. It was my first day of vacation. I'd turned in grades and paperwork and I didn't have to be back at the high school until the end of August. I felt free and easy.

Bear and I made our way down the path that goes from the kitchen, around the garage, to the driveway. From there you can head to the barn and continue down to the mailbox and the road, or you can go the other way to the vegetable garden and the pasture and the woods beyond. It's easier, in dim light, to see the path to the barn. That's where we were headed when I saw a flash of headlights. A car pulled into the driveway and came to a stop about a hundred feet past the gate. When the car cut lights and engine, I instinctively yanked Bear's leash and pulled him into the shelter of the barn.

Squatting next to the dog, I hooked a few fingers under his collar to restrain him and gently wrapped my other hand around his muzzle. I peered around the opening, squinting until I could make out the silhouette of someone moving toward the barn. A flashlight flicked on, aimed at the ground. A circle of light illuminated a pair of dirty boots and blue jean legs. From the stride and size of the figure, I was sure it was a man. I was about to shout something like "Who goes there?" when the figure halted. Even in the half-light, I could see him lifting something to his lips.

Next thing, Bear was whining and squirming like a fish on a hook. I couldn't hold onto the damn dog. He leaped forward and took off. I didn't think twice and ran after him. The intruder took off too. Now, I might've been a history teacher but I played on the varsity football team in high school and college and I've kept in shape since. So I not only caught up with the dog, I made a grab for the guy's jacket, tugging it hard enough to unbalance him. I lowered my shoulder and drove into him. Would've made old Coach Bergstrom proud. The guy fell to the ground and stayed there, gasping for breath. That's when Bear leapt on him, whining and taking little nips at the guy's face and hands.

"Get him off me, get him away from me!" the man screamed. I lifted Bear away and got a good grip on his leash, which had been dragging after him all this time. Only then did I get my first good look at the intruder. He was a sharp-faced, sly-looking specimen. There was a burlap bag on the ground nearby.

"Your name's Duke," I said.

"What of it?"

"You've been taking our dogs, haven't you?"

Duke snatched up the bag and scrambled to his feet. He started to edge away. "You can't prove anything," he said. "You try and I'll sue you for attempted murder."

"You're a trespasser," I said. "I have every legal right to defend my property."

Duke's eyes darted back and forth. He turned and ran. When he got to his car, he yanked open the door, jumped in, and pulled the door closed. I heard the clang and clatter of an engine in serious need of a tune-up. He didn't bother turning around. Just jammed on the gas pedal and careened out of the driveway in reverse.

I stood dumbly and watched him go, belatedly recording details in my mind. The car was a '68 Camaro, metallic gray, primed but not painted. Duke was wearing work boots, jeans, and a brown cloth jacket. He'd smelled funny, like rancid meat. I was positive he was Duke, the fellow I'd come across the year before, when I was hiking on Old Blue Mountain. He was leading a pack mule down the trail. Later, one of the Monte Verde kids told me the man was camped illegally on Miner's Gulch. I'd figured he was another harmless crackpot looking for the legendary lost gold mine. Now he was after a different kind of treasure and he certainly wasn't harmless.

I heard Sally yelling my name.

Bear strained against the leash, tail wagging like a metronome. "We're okay," I called but Sally was already there, breathing hard, clutching a hand to her heart. She got more upset when I described the encounter. I admit I felt shook up too, but I was proud of myself. The heroics added a swagger to my step for awhile, especially after my muscles quit aching.

"What do you mean he smelled like spoiled meat?" Sally wrinkled her nose. Suddenly, she bent down and popped back up, holding a baggie of liver treats between thumb and forefinger. "Evidence," she gloated. "Let's go call the sheriff."

I didn't argue. Better for Duke to be in custody so he couldn't sneak back another night. Plus, people would realize Duke was the dognapping culprit and peace would be restored on Legal Creek. I didn't know it was already too late.

At dawn, the same time Bear and I met up with Duke, Laurence Legal killed one of the Monte Verde dogs. Laurence claimed he was awakened by noises and saw the dog in the pasture, chasing horses. The dog, a yellow Lab, belonged to Danny, and it was Danny who found the body, on the commune side of the creek. Naturally, Monte Verde folks and others were convinced Laurence shot the dog in revenge for the dognapped Winkle.

That afternoon, perhaps not to be outdone, Jack Walker shot the Murphys' dog for trespassing. It's a fact Romeo wandered but everyone knew the dog's motives were strictly amorous. When his nose discovered the Walkers didn't have anything interesting in the way of a female dog in heat, Romeo would've ambled on, seeking better opportunity. Luckily, Jack was a bad aim even with a BB gun so it wasn't fatal, but there were enough pellets in Romeo's butt to hurt like hell and he couldn't have been a pretty sight when he showed up on the Murphys' porch.

That night, someone spray-painted "Killer" on the Ayreses' mailbox, the fancy front gate, and their driveway. Just the one word, over and over in blood-red paint.

By the time a deputy sheriff showed up, three days after I called, Legal Creek was sizzling and not from the rising summer temperature. Pro-hippie or old-timer ally, no Legal Creeker wanted to hear my story about Duke.

Luckily, the deputy did. I recognized him soon as I opened the door. "Todd. Todd Cunningham."

"Mr. Shuster." He looked much as he had in high school, tall, thin, energetic.

"Who is it, Jim?" Sally's voice interrupted my inspection.

I shook my head. "What am I thinking? Deputy Todd Cunningham. Please come in."

Todd's face got serious as I told my story. "You're lucky," he said. "He could've had a gun."

Sally and I exchanged a look. We took turns relating the saga of dog shootings, vandalism, and just plain meanness erupting on Legal Creek. Todd's dark eyebrows lifted higher with each detail. He made a lot of notes on a little pad. When we finished talking, he went to his car to call in. When he returned inside, he said he'd reported the new developments and also asked for backup before going to Duke's campsite. Todd, Sally, and I had a pleasant forty-five minute gossip about people we knew in common while we waited.

The second deputy, named Dixon, was a blond hulk. He brought an old mining map of the area. Todd and Dixon took time to study the map, planning their approach and how they'd handle things if Duke was at the site.

"You'll go in the second car," Todd told me. "In the back seat. You'll wear a bullet-proof vest. If Deputy Dixon yells at you to get down, you will get down."

"Why does he have to go?" Sally's voice trembled. I was touched by her emotion and glad she'd asked the question I couldn't ask without sounding like a wimp.

"We need someone who might be able to identify the dogs," Todd said. "That's if we find any up there. A lot of these guys move them soon as possible."

"What does he do with them?" Sally's eyes were wide. I could tell she was dreading the answer.

"This could well be part of a big operation on the West Coast, selling so-called 'strays' to research labs. Some of the popular breeds get resold as pets." Deputy Dixon's matter-of-fact recital made Sally blink, but she didn't cry.

The upshot was I rode in the backseat of Deputy Dixon's green and white sheriff's car, wiping my sweaty palms and hoping the bulletproof vest muffled the enormous sound of my heartbeat.

They wouldn't let me out of the car until they'd made certain Duke wasn't there or lurking in the woods nearby. I walked with Todd to a flimsy plywood shed beyond the campsite. The doorway was covered with a sheet of black plastic. Todd pulled it aside. A terrible stench assaulted us. Todd pulled a handkerchief from his pocket. All I could do was lift an arm and bury my nose in the crook of my elbow. We were greeted by a frenzy of barking. Wire cages lined three walls, stacked one on top of another. Half were empty but thirteen or fourteen dogs were jammed into a few cages.

My eyes watered in the sharp stink. Even so, when Todd aimed his flashlight at the dog in the middle row, I knew I was looking at the Legals' shar-pei. Its head was down, its ears back, and it was hunched submissively.

"Winkle," I said. She regarded me warily. In the same cage, a dog that looked like Toto from *The Wizard of Oz* was barking hysterically. A Doberman in the cage below snarled. I was glad there was wire mesh between us.

"Recognize any others?" Todd still had the handkerchief over his nose.

I scanned the cages, hoping against all odds I'd discover Poet.

"Maybe that one." I pointed at a small dog in a bottom cage with a shrill, frantic bark. Its white fur was matted and the pink collar with fake diamonds was soiled. "I think I saw a flyer for her. I remember the collar."

Poet wasn't there. It made me sick thinking of him and the other dogs caged in the shed. Deputy Dixon didn't offer much comfort. "Looks like they're all female. Probably keeping these for breeding. The others?" He shrugged.

Todd pulled a camera from his pocket and took pictures of the shed. "We can't just release them, you know. I'll call for help."

I obeyed his order to back out of the shed. Outside, I took a series of deep breaths, as much to gulp oxygen as to keep from losing breakfast. I waited with the two deputies until volunteers from the animal shelter showed up to load the dogs into a couple vans. One of the volunteers discovered a trashcan in the shed, filled with dog ID tags and licenses. The deputies impounded it for evidence, so I couldn't rummage through to look for Poet's tag. Later, Todd told me it wasn't there.

Sally was worried sick until I returned. I was astonished I'd been gone six hours. I started to give Sally a precise description of my day but she interrupted me.

"Wait. I have to know what's going to happen to the dogs."

"They have to be quarantined. Meanwhile, they're trying to match dogs with owners. Some of the dogs have microchips and with the tags they found and all the flyers, they think it'll be pretty easy."

"Imagine the happy reunions." Sally's eyes rimmed with tears. I knew she was thinking of Poet. I took her in my arms to console her. Bear had a different plan. Damn dog came scampering into the room, skidded to a halt at Sally's feet, and looked up at her with doggy adoration. Sally couldn't resist those eyes, the color of dark chocolate. She included Bear in our hug. Not my idea of romantic, I told Sally, having a puppy with suspicious breath lick my face. She gave me a little smile, but she put the dog down, and things progressed according to my original calculation.

Later, I told her what Todd and I planned while we waited for the dog rescue volunteers. "We'll use the school gym," I explained, "keep the dogs in the locker room and bring them out one at a time. Everyone on Legal Creek, Misery Flats, and Keebler Road is being invited. The idea is to reunite dogs with owners but also neighbors with neighbors."

It wasn't the miracle I'd hoped for, but the Yalta Conference near the end of World War II didn't bring world peace either. Still, it made some difference for Ellie Oldham to watch Layla, Jacob, and Star, all commune kids, rolling on the floor with laughter while a little Yorkie skittered around them, licking faces and yapping delightedly. I was touched myself to watch Laurence and Verlie Legal when Winkle was handed into their arms.

The Dog War was over, yet things never went back to how they were. The Ayreses sold their house and moved back to Orange County. By the late '80s, the Monte Verde commune split up, although some of the original residents continue to live on the property. The Murphys moved on. The rest of us no longer gather for New Year's Day road parties, impromptu potlucks or summertime bring-your-own-meat barbecues. We wave at familiar cars. We say hello if we see each other at the market, at the Wineglass Valley Fourth of July celebration, or the fire department's annual rummage sale. Or at funerals.

Jack Walker went five years ago. This spring, Laurence Legal passed away. I'm glad I resolved things with Laurence a few years back. We bumped into each other at the Ace Hardware store out on the highway. Probably it was the plumbing supplies aisle because I'm forever fixing cracked pipes and dripping faucets in our old house. As I recall, Laurence and I both stopped short. And then, without knowing I was going to until I did it, I reached out and offered my hand. A moment or two ticked by before he gripped my hand and gave it a good firm shake.

We didn't say much to each other. Laurence asked about Sally and I asked after Verlie. I watched him walk away, toward the checkout counter, and returned to my search for the right size pipe coupling. Used to be, this stuff was made of metal. Now it's plastic. They just don't make them the way they used to. I'll probably be patching those pipes again in a few more years.

Left Right Wrong

Domi Shoemaker

SITTING IN THE FRONT not-driver's seat of the car. Just Mom and me. The sky-blue, green-on-the-inside car. The sky matched the car's outside, but inside the car it felt like rain.

This was just a few weeks after Dad had moved out. Mom said Dad had already taken everything. I guess when you think everything is what you don't have any more, there's always more something to be took.

That day, the sky-blue sky day, Dad was taking the car to give to his new wife.

Dad's new wife, my mom's old best friend.

Dad's new wife, my old best friend's mom.

Dad's new family, my old best friend's mom, and Mom's old best friend with Dad's new baby on the way.

I didn't know it was the last time for me and Mom and sky-blue car. Dad had been gone since the Fourth of July. Just before my fourth birthday. Fireworks everywhere. Baby was supposed to come at Christmas.

Dad said he needed the car so New Wife could get groceries for New Family. We needed to get groceries, too. Mom, me, and my three brothers, Ron Jon, Nate, and Blake. Dad's old family. Except Ron Jon didn't need groceries on account of he died before he was ever born. But he was still family. I wondered if Ron Jon would stay with us or be in Dad's new family. Maybe both, since he didn't take up no room.

Seemed like our one car needing was more than his new family's two car needing with just them three. Even counting Ron Jon, and even with one more baby coming, you'd think they would have been okay with just their one car. Besides Dad's new baby wasn't around yet, and who was to say it'd make it here alive? Even if it did, it'd take up less room than me.

Car needing didn't have a whole lot to do with car keeping.

Me and Mom, we were best friends. I cried when she cried, but never in the same room. So she didn't know. I wasn't supposed to know, either. Not about the wads of blacked-up mascara toilet paper in the bathroom garbage. Or the soggy and singed Kleenex in the glass ashtray on her nightstand. Or the scrap of napkin poking out of her bra when she came to tuck me in.

My brothers said stop blubbering, but that just made me cry more.

Mom was driving. Me, four, in the front not-driver's seat. My hand palms were open looking at each other, and me looking back and forth between them and Mom. Mom in her pink frost lipstick. Her dyed black hair pulled back tight. Her curly black miniature wig bobby-pinned to the crown of her head. The wig called a Topper, strapped in with Mom's favorite scarf. Mom called it a Silky. We always liked to name things. I was trying to remember my hands' names.

Right hand was easy.

"Right," I said.

Looking at other hand, nothing.

I started over. You always go with what you know first, and the rest will come along.

"Right," I said.

Usually if I concentrated hard enough and asked real nice, just about anything would tell me its name once I had learnt it. I had learnt hand names at Sunday School, but this one wasn't about to give.

"Mom," I said and held out the hand whose name is Right. "If this one is my right," I held the other hand out. "Is this one my wrong?"

Mom laughed and laughed and didn't stop laughing until her laugh was all run out. Then she pulled the car over next to the curb. Kept the engine on. Wasn't much traffic and we just sat there for a minute. Mom's hands on the steering wheel.

She reached over and wrapped her hand around the hand whose name I couldn't remember. "No, silly," Mom said. "This one's not Wrong."

Mom's voice so TV-mom soft. Soft like I hadn't ever heard.

"That one over there," she said. "That one is your right hand . . ."

She was smiling the way she does when just one side of her mouth lifts up and she is not quite finished with the sentence, but I interrupted anyway.

"Mom, I know this one's name," I said, holding Right up in front of my face.

"Ah, yes," Mom said. "I guess you do, Miss Smarty Pants." She held on to Other hand and squeezed. "This one's name is Left."

"Oh, yeah," I said. "Left."

Then Mom, she turned sideways toward me in the front seat that is the driver's seat. I turned sideways to face her. Her pink frost lipstick, green and gold eye shadow sparkling beneath the outline of drawn on eyebrows, and dark pink powder she put on her cheeks. I wanted the whole world to be colored in just like her.

Mom brought Right and Left together in her hands.

"Right, the hand you color with," Mom said. "And Left, the one that helps Right. Just like you help me." Mom pulled Left and Right up to her face, one on either side, and held them there. Closed her eyes.

"Left," I said again. "Like Dad left."

Mom's eyes opened and her underneath eyelids filled up with tears. Tears right about ready to pour over the edge. I wondered if I could make my eyes cry but not spill. Better to wonder about one single thing than to worry about what's coming next.

Mom's eyes got so big and so dark, they sucked in all the sound and most of the light, then looked over my head and out into nowhere. I breathed slow. Stayed still as I could. Terrified that the dark in her eyes might take me in and swallow me up whole, and we'd both be gone forever.

But I had to pee. I brought my knees up and squeezed them together.

Mom closed her eyes and looked down. Everything in her spilled all over my hands. So much heat and so much black, I tried to take my hands back, but she used the palms of Left and Right to wipe off her face. My shoulders started to burn, being pulled like that. I let myself go limp and swallowed me back into myself as much as I could. Mom dabbed her eyelashes with the backs of my hands. No Kleenex, no napkin, no toilet paper.

"Uncle," I said.

Mom let go of my hands, but they didn't feel like mine anymore.

She looked straight ahead the whole way home.

"Left," I said. "Right."

The Blue Jackpot
Gregg Kleiner

DAD WOKE ME EARLY, whispering my name real close. "Chessie. There's a blue jackpot out there. Blooming all the way over." He paused, his coffee breath warm in my ear and nose. I knew what was coming next, even though I didn't want to hear it, ever. "Just what she wanted, your mom. What we've been waiting for. So rise and roll, kiddo. Today's the day, I'm afraid."

After Dad left, I lay in bed listening to my heart loud in my throat and him in the next room waking my big brother, Jake. A few minutes later, Aunt Maureen in her yellow robe walked past my open doorway. She was headed to the bathroom from the guest room where she'd been staying since it happened. She looked so much like Mom going by I almost called out, but caught myself. After Aunt Maureen peed and flushed, I could hear water moving in the pipes. That was when I decided to wear my new swimsuit underneath my long, flowery skirt and my white blouse with the lace on the cuffs and collar. Mom had liked lace, and the suit was all shimmery and blue—her favorite color. And she'd bought the suit for me just before the last time we went to the pool.

When the red canoe was tied on top of the Volvo and Dad and Jake and Aunt Maureen and me were all sitting inside the car, Dad twisted around and put the white box on the back seat between my legs and told me to keep it from tipping over. Mom was in the box. I was holding her on top of my flowery skirt, between my thighs, one palm on each side. The box was heavy, which surprised me because I thought ashes were light and fluffy like dust. The seat was stained where I had dropped a few chocolate chips last summer on the way to the pool with Mom. The chocolate had melted into the seat fabric against my butt skin below where the new blue swimsuit stopped. I didn't know until I'd gotten out at the pool parking lot and touched the gooey mess. At first I thought I'd somehow pooped my-self. But then I knew what it was. Mom helped me wipe the chocolate off my leg and the seat with napkins from the glove box. None got on my new suit. Then Mom and I walked toward the pool in the sun, Mom holding my hand, our fingers sticky. I didn't care. Looking back now, I wouldn't of cared if it had been poop. That's what people do at the very end. I know that now. They can't help it. I helped Dad clean Mom up quite a few times, including at the end.

But that day at the pool was still summer, before fall came, and then the end. Mom was wearing a yellow scarf tied around her head and I was thinking how she wouldn't need a swim-ming cap now, but how the water would run right down into her eyes because her eyebrows were gone, too.

It's weird the stuff you remember, some things clear as wa-ter, like that day at the pool, or the ride the morning of the blue jackpot up to Indigo Lake, to where Mom wrote that she want-ed us to do it.

THE DRIVE SEEMED TO take forever: Aunt Maureen in Mom's seat pushing at her eyes with a gob of white Kleenex. Dad look-ing over at her now and then, his eyes in the rearview mirror glancing back at me. Jake sitting beside me with his head against the window, his hair making the glass greasy. And me in the middle where I always sat because I got carsick and could look out between the front seats. Me and my skirt holding the box in the middle of the Volvo, the red canoe tied above us with the tip poking out over the hood pointing the way. And higher up and all over—all that sky. Mom's blue jackpot. The first one since the service. Just how she wanted.

My heart was still going hard because I didn't want to get to the lake and have to open the box and let her go. But that's what she wanted, so that's what we were driving along toward doing. She'd written it all out: *The first blue jackpot after I'm gone. Up at Indigo Lake. My favorite place in this world. With all of you in the canoe, in the sunshine. I can see it now. A painting. That makes me happy. Let me go!*

We camped at Indigo Lake every summer as a family. Mom would bring all sorts of special treats. Hot chocolate in those little packets, a bag of big marshmallows for s'mores, cold cereal in miniature boxes we'd cut open on the side and pour milk into and eat it that way right out of the box. Lucky Charms, Cocoa Puffs, the kinds of cereals we weren't allowed to have at home. We'd all sleep in an old Army tent, but Mom was always the first one up and out in the mornings. I was second, and I'd find Mom sitting on a big log down by the lake with her coffee, looking out at the water and mountains and sky. I'd crawl up onto the log next to her and she'd put an arm around me and we'd just sit there together in the morning, quiet all around. One time Mom whispered, "We've got ourselves a blue jackpot brewing up there, Chessie." When I asked her what a blue jackpot was, she swept a hand out. "Why, all that blue's what. Not a cloud in sight. A lucky day!" That was the morning Mom and I went in skinny dipping, before breakfast, and before Dad and Jake were up, the two of us swimming below the blue jackpot, swimming through it, too, because the blue was all over the water, the water cool between my legs. I could hear Mom's breathing and her laughing clear as could be coming across the smooth-flat surface of the lake and into my ears. Afterward, sitting back on the log in the sun, both of us wrapped in one big towel, lake water hanging in our hair, Mom whispered, "There's nothing in life quite like a polar bear skinny dip below a blue jackpot, Chessie. This can be our secret, how about? Just us girls."

DAD WAS LEANING FORWARD and craning his neck above the steering wheel to see up past the canoe. "Just look at that sky, will you? Like somebody vacuumed it off. Every last cotton ball whiff of cloud sucked away slick as a whistle." Dad was good at taking your mind off things, saying stuff different, being up-beat, always seeing the good somehow, even in the bad.

Nine years older than me, Jake had been coming back from college a lot that fall. He'd made it home in time on Mom's last day and hadn't gone back yet, since we were waiting for a blue jackpot—rare in Oregon by early October. But we finally had one, and we were riding along underneath it, the four of us left, all family, and Mom, too.

I wanted Dad to turn on the radio because it was so quiet in the car. Just Aunt Maureen snuffling a little, Jake's head bump-ing against the smudged window, Dad's eyes in the mirror, and me there in the middle. All of us alive, and Mom between my skinned knees from when I fell skipping rope fast as I could out in front of our house where the sidewalk is busted by roots from the sweet gum pushing up.

AT THE LAKE, DAD shut off the engine. We sat in the quiet for awhile, nobody moving or saying anything. I don't think any of us wanted to do what Mom wrote. I doubt she knew how hard it would be when she wrote it out. But at last, Dad opened his door and got out, and then Jake did, too, and they untied the canoe and carried it down to the water, along with the paddles.

I stayed in the car, sitting behind Aunt Maureen, my mother's only sister, who looked even more like Mom from behind, their hair the same color, but Aunt Maureen's shorter. I got out and opened the door for Aunt Maureen and the two of us walked down to the water, but she didn't hold my hand, because I was carrying Mom.

We all got into the canoe and Dad paddled us out on the lake. The leaves were turning yellow and red and some floated on the water like little paper stars we paddled through. The sun was warm on my face even though the air was chilly, and the sky was blue just the way Mom wanted it to be. The painting. A little mist rose up off the water here and there, like clouds being born, and everything so still, no campers this late in the year. When we got out a ways, Dad stopped paddling and I knew it was time. I watched the drips falling off the end of his paddle, each drop flashing in the sun as it fell, and then a little blurp in the water. We drifted along, the four of us and Mom, nobody saying a single word. Just the hush of morning below the blue jackpot. The smooth-flat water. All of us breathing. A duck flew over and I could hear its wings pushing the air, see the sun on the underside of its belly.

When Dad started talking, his voice was real quiet. "Why don't we each spread a little to start with," he said. "Chessie, you want to open it and go first?" I didn't want to, but I did it. For Mom. I lifted up the flaps then untwisted the plastic bag that was fastened with a twist-tie like the ones that come on bread bags. But when I saw the gray sand inside, I couldn't do it. I just couldn't. So I passed the box to Dad, who took it, then threw a handful out over the water the way you throw a Frisbee, but real gentle like. The ashes spread out all over, a fine layer floating on the surface, some pieces sinking through the green water, a little dust hanging in the air. Dad handed the box to Jake, and Jake and Aunt Maureen each took a handful and threw them out over the water, too. All around us, the water was dusty, cloudy. Then the box was back to me, but it was still almost full. I took a handful and held it and thought about the melted chocolate chips and Mom's sticky hand. I held my hand out over the side of the canoe and opened it slow until my hand was empty and dry and chalky feeling.

I lifted the box to pass it back to Dad, but the box slipped and hit the side of the canoe and fell into the water. I leaned and tried to grab the box fast but the canoe tipped and I went in, too. Underwater, I opened my eyes quick. I could see the white box sinking away through the green water that was full of sunlight, a blurry trail of ashes and bubbles coming up out of where the flaps were open and waving a little. I started to swim down after the box, but then the box was out of sight, so I stopped, floated there below the dark mark of the canoe above.

When I came up, gasping, everything sparkled. Dad and Jake reaching for me. Aunt Maureen with her white Kleenex over her mouth. The lake water on my lashes. My blue suit bright where it was showing through my wet blouse. My flower skirt floating open on the water all around.

"She's gone!" I cried. "I couldn't get her."

"It's okay, Chessie," Dad said, grabbing my hand. "You did just what she wanted."

BACK HOME, WHEN I got out of my damp suit, I found grit down there. Just a few grains. But it was enough.

Walking Through the Forest with My Mother

Kathleen Lane

SHE'S TALKING ABOUT THE pears again. My mother in the kitchen in a loose lavender shirt I don't like, it's too loose, it should hold her in more.

"Did you see the pears Catherine sent from California?" she says, her face also too loose, it should hold her in more.

Now she will say, "They wrap each one in foil."

"They wrap each one in foil," she says.

I'm buttering toast for our breakfast because toast I understand. You slice the butter, you put it on the toast, you spread it around. It melts.

My "oh really" is not that nice, I know it should have a question mark not a sigh at the end.

"Each one is individually wrapped," my mother says. "I'll go get them."

She leaves the skillet with onions already the color of sap, goes away to fetch the box of pears. I turn off the stove and eat the toast that's supposed to be for the breakfast table. I eat it and it gets stuck in my throat and there she is with that box. With all those pears. Wrapped in foil, packed in foam.

It's a lot of trouble for a pear, isn't it? That's what I want to say. I want to complain about people who ship fruit across the country. Shipping pears across the country is a fucking horrible thing to do. And where is Adam? Where is he now? Did he fly all this way to take leisurely showers? To lather his cheeks with shaving cream? Did I convince him to come home so he could leave me here in the kitchen, alone, while he sits in a chair and drinks his coffee, talking with our dad about what's up and down in the market, and maybe that's how they see Mom's decline, as a temporary dip in value.

"Here," my mother says, peeling the last foil off a pear. Holding it out to me in her hand that looks like her hand, same hand, garden fingers, math teacher fingers, mom fingers. "Try one. You won't believe how sweet they are. Catherine sent them from—"

"California," I say. And know, I know, I know I shouldn't have.

I try to soften, I say, "Was it California?"

I take the pear, bite into it without slicing, without washing. Let the juice hang from my chin. She doesn't protest like the mother who once did, who said *Were you kids raised by apes?* as we picked the blackened skin off turkeys, as we ran our pinkies along the bottoms of cakes, plowing up frosting.

It's one of my tests. I am testing her neurons, which ones were spared in the most recent clear-cutting. The neuron forest, that's what they call it, this place in the brain. Cottontails and knotted pines, you would think. Alzheimer's as some kind of Paul Bunyan.

We walk among the stumps, my mother and I, and occasionally come upon one the ax missed. Running down the hill at Uncle Gary's chicken farm, it's still there. Only split down the middle, my story without me. Now it's Adam in the rain boots and all that mud. It must be the rain outside that's reminded her. It blows against our dining room window at an angle that makes it seem as if someone is standing on the lawn throwing buckets of water at the glass.

We have taken our places at the table. Mom and Dad at the far ends. Across from me, Adam, already reaching for toast, unaware apparently that he has just stolen my story from me. Will he steal my dress, too, the white one I turned gingham with blue marker? Will it be his cheek our mother pats when she says, *And how could I yell at a little girl singing "Somewhere Over the Rainbow"*? Will he become The Howling Wind who forgot to howl in the third-grade play and so was known forever after as The Scowling Wind? My stories, mine. And who will I be then? The six-year-old boy with the pencil behind his ear? Will I wear a dress shirt to the one high school basketball game I ever attended, and when my mother says, *You just never wanted to go out*, will I pretend it was a choice, pretend I wanted to stay home, that school wasn't a hateful place, that I had friends. Oh Adam, I know it was never easy for you.

But for now, we keep our places. Adam with his back to the window. My view over his shoulder of holly and neighbor's fence. Between us, a spread of familiar dishes in various states of completion. A fruit salad of sliced bananas garnished with sliced bananas. A platter of bacon that could have used another ten minutes. Caramelized onions, my whole life a topping to scrambled eggs, have become a dish unto themselves.

"Remember," my mother says to Adam, as if the word is still hers, "how you came flying down that hill? Flew right out of your—

"Not gloves," she says to her juice glass, so quietly, a private matter between the two of them. "Gloves you put on your hands."

I take a bite of banana so I won't say boots. Dad makes busy work of eggs.

"Boots, Ma," Adam says and pokes up a piece of pink ba-con. It hangs from his fork like a wound. Adam who calls our mother's condition forgetfulness. He has convinced my father of this, too.

"Boots," my mother says, "that's right. Your boots got stuck in the mud and you—"

Her eyes move from Adam over to me and like that I'm back in my story. I am me and Adam is Adam, and our mother, she is back, too, laughing her easy laugh, it's just her.

"You," she says, her gums showing how they do when the laugh gets too big for her face. "You," she says, and we're all laughing now, Dad with a mouthful of onion, even Adam—how I used to love to make our math boy laugh, and how many Adams I have dated since, never learning. "You ca-a-," she says. "You ca-a-a-ame up out of that mud looking just—looking just like a-ha-ha-ha—like a-ha-hah-ha—like a little pickaninny!"

And the tree stands tall.

Over the years my mother had learned to say black man. Not coloreds, we corrected, and it's even better if you say African American, but African American was one step too many away from her Darlington porch swing.

The word sits on our table and there is no easy way to brush it away. Even my mother seems confused by it, her laughter less sure, her eyes widening, emptying, until they are nothing but sea glass passing over us, and I wonder, can she see lost in our faces the way we can see it in hers? How we try to stretch our laughter, keep it going, bring it down easy. How we all sud-denly need something passed. Syrup, salt, butter. "Send those potatoes down here will you, sweetie?" my father says. Because this we can do. Hands, potatoes.

My mother makes useless jabs at the onions on her plate. It seems she's addressing the tines when she says, "What's a pickaninny?"

Adam looks at me, as if I had asked it. As if he is angry at me for asking it, though I know it's not me or Mom who's upset him, but this disruption in logic. "A black person," he says.

"African American," I say, not meaning to, but sometimes I go with her, and it's 1985 and I'm fourteen. My hair is pink, my necklaces are weapons, and it's African American.

"It doesn't matter," Adam says in that tone I remember from high school, *why can't you act normal.* Those serious eyes. So serious even when we were young. Claiming banker, priest, the catch-all "boss" in our childhood games, and up until a certain age I believed him. Maybe I still do, maybe that's my problem. I am waiting for Adam to draw me a crayon chart, indicate in blue line and arrow what we're supposed to do now, make mother into pie chart and leave out not one thin sliver.

"It does matter," I say, because it does. Because I realize that everything has always mattered more to me than to Adam, and right now this burden of caring is too much.

We are strangers, Adam and I. I realize this, too. There is forest and river and cliff between us. Some distances are made by birth and some by drift and I can't say which of these, ocean or desert, mother or brother, is harder to cross.

"You kids are going to have to learn to get along," my mother says. Words from back then, from our childhood, how many times. Or does she mean now. Does she mean when. When she's not here, when it's just us.

I look at my mother looking at rain. At Adam curling a cold brown onion on top of his last bite of bacon, he always could eat anything. My father, who looks exhausted by the act of eating, I can hear his breathing across the table, a stormy chested old man's breathing, not the father who taught me to change sails, and what a lonely place is family.

Sometimes I imagine us as islands. Me, Dad, and Adam. Three islands reachable only by my mother, our ferry to one another, and I think, my God, when she goes, what then?

"Pass the—" my mother says to me, "—that there," she

says, waving a finger at the toast I buttered and stacked like brick and mortar. Enough toast for ten, not four, but it never looked like enough on the plate. I wanted higher.

My dad hands the plate to her but he has seen something in my eyes and he is not one to tolerate sadness. Unhappiness is not something we do. "Hey kiddo," he says, "did I tell you they're building a new park down along the waterfront?"

"No," my mother says, "I don't believe you did."

My charming mother. My lovely mother. With fork and knife, making steak of toast.

Her words, so sweet, so sudden and wrong, have caught my dad and Adam, too. No time to pretend, to change the subject, reach for salt. I've already seen it in their eyes, in their tight smiles they hold too long.

My dad looks down at his empty plate, still that smile, but I can see his lips won't hold for long. This is what I wanted, right? To bring my dad and Adam with me to this awful place, but why then do I now want to take it all back? Tell my dad that I was wrong, that everything is okay. It's only forgetfulness. I want to tell Adam to pick up his fork, keep eating. Have that last onion. Here, take my bacon.

I put my hand on top of my mother's fingers that have already begun their curl into grapevine, and listen to my dad take a slow deep breath.

I don't know how many times he's told my mother about this park on the waterfront, but by the uncharacteristic flatness of his voice, I would guess more than a few. But my father is also a storyteller, through and through, and by the time he gets to the three miles of bike path, he is, once again, the self-proclaimed bag of wind who charmed my mother into marrying him by skating her around a frozen pond until she lost feeling in her legs. It's as if he's truly forgotten every past telling when he describes for her the covered picnic areas, the fountain designed by some Greek fellow out of Minneapolis, the concerts they'll have right down there by the water.

"Well, doesn't that sound nice," my mother says.

"Sure does, Ma." My brother, suddenly a person who says *sure does*. He winks a sweet little sad little one-eyed blink at me. My brother, a winker now, too.

Later, after the dishes have been cleaned and put away, the neighbor stops by to meet us. She is a new neighbor and doesn't suspect anything, doesn't notice how softly we speak now, how lightly we walk, and when my mother goes to fetch the pears, they are only pears. They are only pears sent from California. Wrapped in foil, packed in foam, "the sweetest pears you'll ever taste," my mother says, and I try I try I try to swallow their juice and smile.

A Good Crack and Break

Joanna Rose

Leo Gregorsky, who owns The Dublin, favors the music of his youth back in Cleveland—John Cougar Mellencamp, Bob Seger. Good bar noise. Sometimes he plays Steve Miller and the old local boys get to singing. Sometimes, when the heavy door opens between songs, maybe blows back and hangs there on the hinges, and the loud quiet of a rainy Northwest night gets in, someone yells to shut the damn doors, or maybe put on some more tunes. It's that kind of place, especially in the winter. Folks spend more time in The Dublin in winter. It's dark by four thirty, rainy season, and work slows down.

Monday afternoons are quiet and Ellen Tanner was working the bar. Leo sat in the corner with Bob, the Budweiser driver, who saves The Dublin until the end of his route for the sake of sitting back and having one with Leo. The two of them filled up the corner with easy, gray-haired bulk.

"That little Ellen worked at the diner in Chinook," is what Bob had to say.

"Used to sell used cars before that."

"That so?"

"Longview."

"Hm."

She was behind the bar, flipping through CDs, and Roy Al was playing video poker, and Danny Green was working a shot of bourbon at the bar. The place hadn't started filling up yet, old Toby was anchored at his own end of the bar, some guys were playing pool, it was still early, and a guy came in and left the door open. He walked up to the end of the bar in work boots thick with mud, shrugged out of a wet green Carhartt jacket, and dropped it on the stool next to him.

It was one of those between-songs moments, and Roy Al got up and shut the door and said, "Asshole," but Roy Al had his teeth in his pocket and when he has his teeth in his pocket no one can tell what he's saying.

The guy ordered a martini, neat.

Ellen said, "You mean like *up*?"

The guy leaned back and dug a wallet out of his jeans. "Don't put it in one of those fag glasses." His voice wasn't too low, and it wasn't too respectful. "Just put it in a glass without ice."

Leo drained his beer. There aren't any fags in Grays River, except during the summer, the kayakers down from Seattle and the SUVs full of hikers and whatnot, but still, folks are respectful about such things in this day and age. Even old Toby, who's been parked at the end of the bar drinking cold coffee for fifteen years, knows that. Leo studied the foamy trails inside the empty glass. Roy Al would be snickering in his nasty little brain. Danny Green drank down his bourbon and circled the shot glass with his big knuckled hands.

Ellen put the rocks glass with the martini down in front of the guy. It had an olive on a toothpick sitting in it. She looked at it for a second and then grabbed a napkin and slid it under there.

She said, "That look like what you had in mind?"

Ellen is a sweetheart, a little on the round side, with a

squeaky voice and a nervous giggle. Known to be kindhearted with the drinks when you're out of work.

The guy took the olive on the toothpick out and set it on the bar.

"Just a drink," he said. "All's I want."

Ellen hit the play button on the stereo, John Hiatt, that song about the haunted house. She likes that one, plays it over and over sometimes until someone says, Come on, babe, give it a rest, and then it'll usually be Bonnie Raitt. She isn't one of your Joni Mitchell types.

Danny Green turned his back on the guy with the martini. There was a nine-ball game going on. Danny was a hot shot in high school, like most guys, playing the full-size tables at the rec center but he doesn't play much pool any more. He doesn't throw darts or play bar dice, and he doesn't sit around and complain about the rain or the work or the lack of work. He goes hunting alone and fishes a bend up Deep Creek and no one else fishes that stretch of the creek whether his truck is there or not.

The guy slammed his empty rocks glass on the bar. It was the kind of sound that got folks' attention on a boring rainy night. "Think you can make another one?" he said. "Leave the salad out?"

John Hiatt sang out his woe and Danny Green turned back around to the bar.

"Have another one, Bob?" is what Leo said.

"Believe I will."

Leo held two fingers up, and Ellen drew two more beers, tipped off the foam, she never has gotten the hang of a new keg, and then she took them to the table in the corner.

Leo said, "Ellen, when you gonna sell me that Duster of yours?"

Ellen giggled her giggle. "I will never sell that Duster, Leo." She picked up Bob's empty glass. "One of Detroit's greatest hits."

She went back behind the bar, adding, "A straight six with 20,000 original miles," over her shoulder, making it sound like it was a song she was singing.

She made the guy his martini, left the salad out, set it gently on the napkin, kind of humming along with John Hiatt. The door opened, the guys from the overpass project came in, there was the rain, a semi gearing down, the afternoon moving on.

The guy laid some bills on the bar. He said, "How about I pay up?"

Roy Al mumbled, "Yeah, how about you pay up?" Two of hearts, five of spades ding dinging on the video poker machine.

Ellen took the bills and turned to put them in the cash register, and she said, "Y'all take care, it's a nasty one out there."

The guy said, "Like I asked for a weather report."

She didn't bother to turn back around. Didn't even look in the mirror behind the bar and watch him down his drink and then leave.

"Managed to shut the damn door," was what Roy Al said.

Danny told Ellen he was buying Roy Al's next Seven and Seven and she said, "Roy Al doesn't need any next one."

Old Toby lit a cigarette off the one he already had going, and three guys shouted over the nine ball going down. Danny looked past Toby, out the window, watched the guy tear out of the parking lot in a dark colored three-quarter ton Chevy.

"It's just a rainy Monday, Danny," was what Ellen said, and she poured him another shot.

FRIDAY NIGHTS IT'S LEO behind the bar and Ellen working the kitchen and Frankie Jones running out sandwiches and delivering drinks to the tables. Frankie is learning the trade. He'd been in Bend and out around Baker City and some other places. Scrawny kid, wears his blue jeans baggy and hanging down, but he hustles that bus tub around and always makes sure folks have the ketchup or hot sauce or coffee or whatnot.

Leo was cutting limes into small wedges.

"See here," he said to Frankie. "Not too small."

Roy Al was slamming dice on the bar with Toby, and the dice game went quiet when the martini guy came in, managed to shut the door this time, walked up to the bar, and told Leo to make him a martini neat. Frankie said, "Wow."

Frankie says wow a lot, no one is quite sure what he means by it. Sometimes he'll be telling some story or relating some incident and he'll end up saying, "It was just, wow." Sometimes it's "Like, wow," as if there are variations on the level of wow.

Leo wiped his hands and said, "Sure thing, friend."

Frankie said, "You gonna use one of those glasses?"

Leo said, "Gentleman ordered it neat, son, not up. Difference there," and he scooped ice into the shaker. Then he pulled out the gin bottle and showed it to Frankie. "They don't say vodka, it's automatically gin." Leo knows about martinis, and Manhattans, and he can whip up just about any blender concoction the summer folks could think of, although it does seem that every new summer brings a new drink along with it. "Now," he said to Frankie. "Here's the important part. The gentleman didn't say dry, so we put just a touch of this in there." Frankie leaned over the bar to get a look at the vermouth, and Leo showed him the label. Ellen likes to refer to their relationship as the edification of Frankie Jones.

The guy said, "What is this, make a drink 101?"

Roy Al snorted and Frankie just let his mouth hang open, which Leo has told him more than once not to do, that it looks unintelligent, and is no way to meet girls. Leo opened the vermouth. Poured just a touch into the shaker, gave the shaker a shake, and poured the martini into a rocks glass.

He set the drink in front of the guy and said, "That be it friend?"

Danny Green came in. He shut the door behind him and stood there, wiping his boots on the thick doormat. When he crosses the floor to the bar, for all his size, you don't feel his footfall on the old floorboards. He'd played one good season in high school, defensive line. He had good feet.

The guy took the drink and gulped it down and set the glass back on the bar. He shrugged out of his wet jacket and he said, "Do it again."

Frankie said, "Wow."

Roy Al slammed the dice cup on the bar and whooped at the roll and Toby lit a cigarette. Old Toby lights a lot more cigarettes than he actually smokes. Roy Al usually finishes them off for him, although otherwise he doesn't smoke himself. Roy Al and Toby go back a long ways.

Leo said, "Frankie, you want to haul me out some more ice?" He didn't say that Frankie should close his mouth too, but Frankie did that anyway. Frankie is no dummy. Maybe a fool, but he's young.

Leo set a shot glass on the bar in front of Danny. Filled it with bourbon.

The three gals who worked up at the senior center came in, laughing already, sat in a booth, and one of them called out, "Hey is Frankie here tonight?" and they all laughed some more and lit up cigarettes and ordered drafts. They were in a booth by a window.

The guy said, "You hear me ask for another one?"

The booths by the windows are the smoking section, including Toby's seat at the end of the bar. You just have to open the windows, no matter how cold it is. All this does is blow the smoke back in, but folks generally believe that No Smoking rules in a bar are nonsense anyway and that the state government doesn't have the right.

The guy put a ten on the bar and said, "Give me some quarters for the pool table too."

Danny drank his shot and set the shot glass down on the bar with a hard, round, empty sound.

Leo said, "They going down easy tonight, Danny?"

And he poured Danny another. Then he lined three beer glasses up under the tap.

Roy Al wiggled around on his stool down there by Toby. He had his teeth in his mouth tonight.

Danny said, "Seven and Seven down there," and Leo said, "Sure thing."

Roy Al's latest lady friend came in with a new hairdo, all curly gray and flipped up around her face, and then some guys from the phone company came in, soaking wet from climbing poles and digging ditches for computer stuff so everybody in the world can have the internet. The science teacher from the Grays River High School came in and dropped his quarters in the pool table. The science teacher loves to play pool. He says it's like evolution and intelligent design all at once, a solid rack, a good crack and break, and the balls go everywhere. The science teacher and one of the phone company guys circled the pool table. Toby stumped over to the video poker machine, leaving Roy Al and his ladyfriend to their business. The Dublin was filling up with smoke and the smell of evening, french fries and burgers and fish baskets. The sound of rain and people ignoring it. There was a soccer game on the TV and Leo wanted to get those captions going across the bottom of the screen. He stared at the remote, front and back. There are some curiosities far beyond him, TV being one of them, although he has no problem with evolution versus this so-called intelligent design. The guy at the bar with his empty martini glass muttered, "Pussy football players in shorts."

Leo turned to the guy. He picked up the guy's empty glass and set it down in the dish rack. He put his big hand flat on the ten-dollar bill. Slid it back to the guy. Then he went down to where Danny was hunched over his bourbon, and he leaned on the bar there, both of them watching the pool game. The noise level wavered between the soccer game, the stereo, the deep fryer, and one of the gals from the senior center hooting at Frankie about his saggy jeans.

The science teacher sank the nine ball on his second shot. That was like, wow. There was the bell sound of the video poker machine, Ellen singing out "Order up, Frankie," and the sweet laughter of the gals from the senior center. The martini guy picked up his ten-dollar bill and his jacket and left, and he didn't shut the big door tight, leaving it to blow back open onto the night, and the rain, and the river out back rising, and the semis on the highway that kept on going toward the coast. Danny stood up. Stepped over to the door and pulled it shut. Came back to Leo at the bar.

"Yes sir," he said, picking up the shot of bourbon. "Going down easy," and he turned his attention to the new pool game setting up.

Roy Al gently touched his ladyfriend's hair. It wasn't all stiff, just regular curly women's hair.

"Real pretty," he said, which, as luck would have it, was the right thing to say that night.

About the authors

Jan Baross's background is in filmmaking, art, and theater. Her writer's life spans screenplays, journalism, novels, short stories, and travel books and teaching. Her first novel, *José Builds a Woman*, won first place for fiction in the Kay Snow Awards. "The Promised Land" is the first piece in her linked short story collection, *The Bakersfield Diaries*. She posts a sketch a day on her Facebook and blog of happenings around Portland that she attends. Website: janbaross.com.

Gail Bartley, a native Oregonian, moved to Bend from New York City in 1998, where she lives with her husband and rescue Austrian shepherd (Mr. Blue). A writer of fiction, creative nonfiction, and screenplays, her work has appeared in the *Berkeley Fiction Review* and *Carve Magazine*, among others. Her essay, "The Big Indian's Last Stand," was a first-place winner in the 2013 Nature of Words literary festival's Rising Star competition. Her screenplay "Goodnight, Irene" has been optioned multiple times and was one of thirty-five domestic and international projects featured in the 2004 IFP/New York No Borders International Co-Production Market. Also a dancer, choreographer, and painter, she directs a tiny but dedicated dance company (The Jazz Dance Collective) and manages a domestic violence intervention program. She is working on her first novel.

Victoria Blake is a Portland resident, a graduate of the Warren Wilson Program for Writers, and, in a previous life, the founder and publisher of Underland Press. She is the publisher of InFact Books, the imprint from Creative Nonfiction Foundation. For more information, please visit victoriablake.com.

Alisha Churbe lives in Portland, Oregon, but is always planning her next international escape. If you can pry the pen from her hand, Alisha can be found with her splendid husband, their amusing friends, and a delicious meal with wine.

Sage Cohen is the author of the poetry collection *Like the Heart, the World* from Queen of Wands Press and the nonfiction books *Writing the Life Poetic* and *The Productive Writer*, both from Writer's Digest Books. She has won first place in the Ghost Road Poetry Contest and published a variety of articles on the writing life in *Writer's Digest* magazine, *Poet's Market* and *Writer's Market*. Her work has appeared in a wide range of publications, including: *Rattle, Poetry Flash, Hip Mama, Cup of Comfort for Writers, The Sow's Ear Review,* and *Oregon Literary Review.* Sage offers support and encouragement for writers at pathofpossibility.com and for divorcing parents at radicaldivorce.com.

Ellen Davidson Levine wrote her first story at the age of four, a story highly praised by all her relatives. After a successful career as a community college instructor and administrator, receiving state and national awards for excellence, Ellen returned to writing full-time, this time in a studio she built in the woods behind her rural Southern Oregon home. A winner of the Bloomie Award for her short story "My Mother's Closet" and author of *Looking for Karma at the Eden Cafe* and *The Importance of Bulldogs—A Novel*, Ellen has also been published in various education and professional journals and has prepared white papers and reports for the U.S. Department of Education and the Oregon Legislature. She is currently working on a collection of short stories about the (semi) fictional *Wineglass Valley.* Learn more at ellendavidsonlevine.com.

Steve Denniston lives in Portland, Oregon, and works at an elementary school with students who have autism. Whenever he gets the chance he writes, whether it's on a lunch break, at boring (or interesting) meetings, or during conversations with his wife—but that rarely ends well. "Are you listening to me?" "Yes." "Or are you thinking about a story?" "Ummm." "You're thinking about using this conversation in a story, aren't you?" "I'll tell everyone it's fiction, okay? Wait! Come back!"

Trevor Dodge is the author of two collections of short fiction (*The Laws of Average* and *Everyone I Know Lives On Roads*), a novella (*Yellow #10*), and collaborator on the writing anti-text-book *Architectures of Possibility: After Innovative Writing*. He teaches writing, literature, and comics studies at Clackamas Community College and the Pacific Northwest College of Art. He lives in Oregon City and also online at trevordodge.com.

Gregg Kleiner's novel, *Where River Turns to Sky* (HarperCollins), was a finalist for both the Oregon Book Award and the Paterson Fiction Prize. He grew up on creeks outside various small towns in Oregon, including Lookingglass, Langlois, and Silverton, and currently resides near the confluence of the Willamette and Marys rivers. At age sixteen, he spent a year as an AFS exchange student in the mountains of northern

Thailand, where for a month he entered a Buddhist monastery under the tutelage of an aged monk. His just-completed collection of short fiction explores community, elders, and climate change.

Christi Krug's award-winning, soulful, and sometimes devious words have appeared in everything from handmade zines to international magazines, from Sunday School take-home papers to horror anthologies. In addition to several works of poetry, speculative fiction, literary fiction, and memoir, hundreds of her nonfiction pieces have appeared in print and online. Christi is the creator of Wildfire Writing, a workshop she teaches for Clark College and independently, helping writers overcome obstacles. She serves as coach and editor for writers across the country, and hosts a popular short story series at Cascade Park Community Library in Vancouver, Washington. She has brought her inspiration to libraries, camps, retirement homes, retreat centers, elementary schools, and many a kitchen table. For more information, see christikrug.com.

Kathleen Lane's stories can be found in *Swink Magazine*, Chronicle Books, *Poor Claudia, Coal City Review,* and elsewhere. She lives in Portland, Oregon, where she is a visiting instructor at Pacific Northwest College of Art, a writer-in-residence with Literary Arts' Writers in the Schools program, and co-host of the art and literary event series SHARE. You can read more about her at kathleenlane.info.

Dylan Lee's day/night/weekend job is writing advertising copy. (Which is actually quite similar to *Mad Men* and *Bewitched* if you take out the excessive drinking, anything resembling a suit, and most witches.) He's been published in *Fiction Attic* and *Phoebe*. And although he wasn't born in the Pacific Northwest, Portland is the first city he's really felt at home in. Beyond writing, Dylan enjoys spending time with his family, going to Africa on safari, and not dying on safari.

Margaret Malone's work has appeared in *The Missouri Review, Oregon Humanities, Swink, Coal City Review, latimes.com,* and elsewhere. She is the recipient of an Oregon Literary Fellowship and an Oregon Arts Commission Individual Artist Fellowship. A co-host of the artist and literary gathering SHARE, she lives in Portland with her husband and two children. You can learn more about her at margaretmalone.com.

Matthew Robinson lives and writes in Portland, Oregon; studies writing at Portland State University; has had work recently appear at *Split Lip Magazine, Black Heart Magazine, Drunk Monkeys,* and *Word Riot*; and you can find more of his words at matthewrobinsonwrites.com.

Joanna Rose has published poems, stories, essays, reviews, one novel called *Little Miss Strange,* and several pieces that are none of the above. She lives in Portland and teaches here and there, including in her dining room as part of The Pinewood Table group. She has dogs.

Lois Rosen's short stories have appeared most recently in: *Alimentum: the Literature of Food, Calyx, Raven Chronicles,* and *VoiceCatcher.* "Splinters" comes from her completed novel-in-stories, *Junior Lifesaving.* Traprock Books published her poetry book, *Pigeons.* A Salem, Oregon, resident, her writing often transports her back to the New York of her childhood. She's taught creative writing at Willamette University and ESL at Chemeketa Community College. A graduate of Rainier Writing Workshop's MFA program, Lois was awarded a Debra Tall Memorial Scholarship. She's also enjoyed residencies at Soapstone, Vermont Studio Center, the Anderson Center, and Centrum.

Jackie Shannon Hollis grew up on a farm in a small town on the east side of Oregon, where the view was wheat fields and combines. Now she lives in Portland, Oregon, where the view is cedars and the mail truck bringing mail right up to the house. Her work has appeared in various literary magazines, including *The Sun, Rosebud, Inkwell, High Desert Journal*, and *Slice Magazine*. She has completed a novel and is currently working on a memoir. You can see more of her work at jackieshannon hollis.com.

Domi J Shoemaker is an Idaho-raised, Portland-steeped gender-fucker based in Portland, Oregon, and is a card-carrying member of Tom Spanbauer's Dangerous Writing group. Domi has been a youth counselor and crisis intervention specialist, publishing intern at Chiasmus Media, and Collaborative Art Bandit with Lidia Yuknavitch, and is the founder of the Burnt Tongue reading series. Domi's fiction has appeared in *[PANK]* online, *Unshod Quills*, and the literary magazine *Gobshite Quarterly*.

Scott Sparling's novel, *Wire to Wire*, was published by Tin House Books in 2011 and received a 2012 Michigan Notable Book Award. *Wire to Wire* is a story of train hopping, glue sniffing, drug dealing, and love, set in Northern Michigan in the late 1970s. Sparling's work has been supported by the Seattle Arts Commission and the Oregon Arts Commission. He is currently finishing a novel about Occupy, Jimi Hendrix, and organ theft. He lives outside Portland, Oregon, near Sucker Lake and writes in a treehouse.

Tammy Lynne Stoner has been a gas station attendant, a paid volunteer for medical experiments, a waitress at a Greek diner, a roadie for Willie Nelson, and a biscuit maker. Now she writes and teaches college. She earned her M.F.A. from Antioch University, has been published here and there—most recently with *Folio, 10,000 Pounds of Black Ink*, and *Unshod Quills*, who nominated her for a Million Writers Award. In 2012 she was offered a fellowship to the Summer Literary Series in Kenya. In 2013 she and her partner had twins, so currently Tammy is focused on catnaps, swaddling, and moving everything up one shelf. See TammyLynneStoner.com.

Jennifer Williams is a big fan of all things Oregon and she and her daughter live in Portland. She is a graduate of Pacific University's Creative Writing Program, and prior to pursuing a career in writing, she worked as an engineer in Phoenix. This is her first publication.

Cindy Williams Gutiérrez is a poet-dramatist whose Aztec-inspired poetry collection, *the small claim of bones,* is forthcoming from Bilingual Press (Arizona State University). Her work has appeared in *Borderlands, Calyx, Cider Press Review, Crab Orchard Review,* Harvard's *Journal of Feminist Studies in Religion,* the Universidad Nacional Autónoma de México's (UNAM's) *Periódico de poesía, Portland Review, Quiddity, Rain Taxi, Rattle,* and *Zyzzyva,* among others. In 2014, her play, *Words That Burn: A Dramatization of William Stafford, Lawson Inada, and Guy Gabaldón in Their Own Words,* will premiere at the Milagro Theatre in commemoration of the Stafford Centennial and Hispanic Heritage Month. Cindy earned an MFA from the University of Southern Maine Stonecoast Program. She teaches poetry to adults, as well as to youth through the Portland Art Museum, the Right Brain Initiative, Wordstock, and Writers in the Schools. As founder of el Grupo de '08, a Lorca-inspired collaborative artists' salon, she looks forward to pushing the boundaries of creative collaboration with many other Northwest artists in the future.

About the Artist

CLARE CARPENTER IS A letterpress printer, book artist, and illustrator from Portland, Oregon. Her work is heavily inspired by place and how our landscape is imbued with personal histories, often blending narrative with traditional and contemporary print methods. Carpenter is the proprietor of Tiger Food Press, a letterpress print studio in Portland, Oregon. She can be found at tigerfoodpress.com.

About the Editor

LIZ PRATO WAS BORN and raised in Denver, where the mountains are majestic, but everything else is brown and flat. In the eighties, she sported a bleached blond faux-hawk and attended Lewis & Clark College. After college, she worked a series of McJobs, then worked as a nonprofit fundraiser, then became a massage therapist, then got serious about studying the craft of writing.

Liz's short stories and essays have appeared in *Hayden's Ferry Review, Subtropics, The Rumpus, Iron Horse Literary Review, Hunger Mountain, Carve,* and ZYZZYVA, among others. She was the Guest Prose Editor for the Summer 2013 issue of *VoiceCatcher.* Awards include the 2010 Minnetonka Review Editor's Prize, first place in the 2005 *Berkeley Fiction Review* Sudden Fiction Contest, and a scholarship to the 2012 Sewanee Writers' Conference. She began teaching at the Attic Institute in 2008, and has taught creative writing for several literary organizations in Oregon.

Liz lives with furry feline friends and her best friend / husband, who is a bookseller, musician, and writer. And, yes, she still dreams of palm trees. Every day. *lizprato.com*